COLDIRON

Spoils of War

Books by F.M. Parker

Coldiron *series*
Coldiron
Shadow of the Wolf
The Shanghaiers
Thunder of Cannon
Spoils of War (a.k.a. The Thieves)

Novels
Skinner
Nighthawk
The Searcher
The Highbinders
The Far Battleground
The Shadow Man
The Slavers
The Assassins
The Predators
Winter Woman
The Seekers
The Highwayman
The Last Orphan Train
Wife Stealer
The Harvester
Soldiers of Conquest
Dream Hitcher

COLDIRON

Spoils of War

F.M. Parker

SPEAKING VOLUMES, LLC
NAPLES, FLORIDA
2021

Spoils of War
(a.k.a. The Thieves)

Cover design by Hannah Linder

ISBN 978-1-64540-495-8

The Making of the Land
A Prologue

The "Big Bang", as scientists have come to call it, created the universe 14 billion years ago. That immense explosive event brought into existence the three elements necessary to create a universe, matter and space and time. As time passed and matter swept outward creating ever expanding space, it cooled and collected into larger and larger bodies under the influence of gravity – to create galaxies made of solar systems, and planets. And it made moons to move across the heavens above the planets.

One of these mighty galaxies was the Milky Way. On the outer edge of the Milky Way was the Sun, a small gas star, and one of the planets rotating around that sun was the Earth. During many millions of years, the lighter minerals of the molten earth rose to the surface and coalesced into one super, rocky continent standing above the one, great ocean.

Pangaea, the last super-continent, existed up until about 235 million years ago. At that time, an immense upwelling from the interior of the earth broke Pangaea into several pieces. These tectonic plates, these continents, went rafting away upon the hotter, molten layer below and divided the earth's one great ocean into two, the Atlantic and the Pacific. Over the following millions of years, the rocky plates drifted toward their present-day positions.

Seventy million years ago, the huge Pacific Plate moving northwest, collided with an unimaginably force against the North American Plate. The Pacific Plate dove under the lighter North American Continent, lifting and buckling the rocks of its western edge and thrusting them upward into a giant mountain range five miles high and stretching for 3,000 miles north to south.

The high crowns of the mountains brushed the heavens, their jagged spires piercing the clouds that rushed by, ripping open their stomachs to let the rain and snow pour down. On the higher elevations it was very cold and the snow never fully melted from one year to the next, accumulating into glaciers, that slipped slowly, like frigid tears, down the faces of the mountains.

Colder still the world became and glaciers were birthed, even on the low plains. Over tens of thousands of years, they grew together, merging into one colossal glacier over two miles thick. The white mantle of ice, its solid ice crystals turned plastic by its own immeasurable crushing tons, flowed outward slow and cold. It overrode the mountains and lakes to smother a third of the continent. In places the crust of the earth was gouged and pressed down into deep, wide basins.

During millions of years, the glaciers advanced and retreated again and again. In the harsh, frozen part of the cycle, the land was buried under an unbelievably large expanse of ice. Wet, warm pluvial times, the interglacial periods, melted the ice, creating deep lakes and violent torrents that sped off to the sea, scouring the mountains and plains that lay in their path.

Only great animals could survive in such a rugged climate. The giant wide-horned bison, the woolly mammoth and the huge beaver Castoridae, eight feet long with twelve-inch incisors, strode upon the land. They were mighty animals, perfectly adapted to the alternating cold and pluvial eras, and they thrived. Just one enemy, the saber-toothed tiger, could pull them down. The vulture condor matched the scale of the other beasts, gliding down on twelve-foot wings to clear up the scraps after the tiger's kill.

Then a change occurred in the climate, the continental glacier retreated and most of the mountain glaciers melted and the land grew drier and drier. The gigantic bison died, so too did the mammoth, saber tooth tiger, giant beaver and the scavenger condor. The beaver and the bison were replaced with small replicate of their original ancestors.

That is the way a tribe of men migrating with their sturdy women and children, from a far and distant place in the north, reached the south end of the mountains some 13,000 years ago. They called themselves The People. They found the land hospitable with its river and smaller steams and the animals to hunt and they stayed. Their numbers increased with each generation.

Thirteen thousand years later, barely a tick of time as measured on the geologic clock, a small group of a second tribe of men arrived with their women and children. Guarded by soldiers, they made their way cautiously up from the south. This time was 1609 as measured by man's clock. They called themselves Spanish and they also liked the land with its mountains and streams. The Spanish gave the river a name. Rio Grande, and the mountains they called Sangre de Cristo (Blood of Christ) Mountains, and they settled there with their women and children. They named their town Santa Fe.

Time ticked again and a third tribe of men arrived, flowing out from the east and onto the great plains and further still climbing up into the great rocky mountains and onward to the waters of the Pacific Ocean. It was a white skinned breed, warlike and possessive. They called themselves Americans and they made savage war upon the first two tribes.

In April 25, 1846 the Americans invaded Mexico in what history would call "The U.S.-Mexican War (1846-1848)". In that war, the Americans invaded Mexico from the north at Monterrey and from the south by landing from ships at Vera Cruz. They defeated Mexican armies in several fierce battles and occupied that nation's capital, Mexico City.

In 1848, the war ended with the Treaty of Guadalupe Hidalgo. With that Treaty, the Americans forced the Mexicans to surrender half of their nation, all the land north of the Rio Grande. That increased the size of the United States by a third. From that immense land area, the states of Texas, California, Utah, Nevada, New Mexico and Arizona were formed, and parts of several other states. It also settled the question of the boundary between Texas and Mexico, the Rio Grande River.

Chapter One

Moon of Wind, March, 1846
**Fort Polk, US Military encampment on the south side
of the Nueces River where it empties its flow of water
into the Gulf of Mexico.**

General Zachary Taylor awoke on the narrow cot in
the darkness of the army tent. He lay silently and listened
for any sound; any sign that would tell him had the black
night brought danger upon him and his small army
camped upon the land claimed by Mexico, a nation with
an army three times the size of that of the Americans.

The distant call of a patrolling sentry came to Taylor.
Closer to his tent, came the soft snuffle of a horse that
was always tied close by should he need it in a hurry.
Closer still, came the sound of movement, that of his
orderly who always managed to rise before him.

Satisfied that all was secure with his army, he swung
his feet onto the canvas that covered the ground and sat
quietly on the cot. These first few moments of the
morning were his lonely time of the day. To dampen that
loneness, he pulled his fondest memories up from where
they were stored in those secret pockets of his mind. First

among them was his wife Margaret with her gentle words, soft body and loving ways. Second was his plantation of two thousand acres of fertile soil along the Mississippi River near Natchez, Louisiana. He found great pleasure in riding horseback upon his land and watching his eighty slaves plant seeds in the spring and harvest the cotton, tobacco and the corn in the fall.

He was an old warrior who had spent much too much time on assignments far away from those he loved. That absence was coming to an end, for this was the last time he would lead men into battle. Once these battles that loomed close ahead were fought, battles he must win, his wife and land would have his full time presence. Sadly, he would rarely have the pleasant company of his four daughters and son for they were all married and had their own homes.

He rose to his feet, age 62, standing five feet and eight inches tall and strongly built, and dressed in the darkness. He lit the candle on his writing desk and its light illuminated his strongly featured face with its prominent nose, high forehead and full lips. He stepped across the tent to the flap of canvas that served as a door and shoved it aside. A slow westerly wind fanned his face. Far away to the east on the flat, wet horizon of the Gulf of Mexico, a thin streak of golden light heralded the imminent arrival of the sun.

Taylor called to the young orderly standing at his post in the morning dusk and watching him. "Trooper, go the officers' mess and tell the chief cook to send my coffee. And tell him it had better be hot or I'll skin him."

"Yes, sir."

"Then find General Worth and tell him that I would like his presence at his earliest convenience." General Worth was one of the three generals that commanded portions of Taylor's army, and the most skilled of the three.

"Yes, sir." The trooper left with long, swift strides toward the officers' mess not far distant.

Taylor focused on the army encampment taking form in the growing daylight. From his elevated position above the beach, the camp was visible stretching for a mile along the shore of the gulf. On the broad, flat sand beach just above high tide, two parallel rows of tents, five hundred in each, sheltered his 4,000 troopers. That number was greater than half of the entire American army of 7,400 troopers. Next inland were the mess tents, then the tents serving as hospitals, then the neat rows of cannon on their wheeled carriages and then the scores of wagons needed to transport all provisions for his army. Further inland were pastures for the hundreds of big draft horses and another one for the slender mounts of his Dragoons.

Taylor turned to the orderly that came hurrying with a large mug of coffee. He nodded to the orderly, took the coffee and entered the tent.

He seated himself at his writing desk, had a long drink of the coffee and placed it on the desk. He took up the report he had prepared for President James Polk and read what he had written to described the condition of his army and his plan of action. Satisfied with the report's contents, he folded it, picked up the candle and dripped several drops of the melted wax to seal it from prying eyes. He inserted it into an official military mail pouch and locked it with a key; identical copies of which both the president and the secretary of war possessed.

Cuddling the hot mug of coffee between his hands, Taylor reviewed the events that had brought him to this encampment. In July the year past, President James Polk had summoned him to Washington. There he had met with the President and William Marcy, Secretary of War. The President, an intense, assertive man, had spoken with fervor and at length about the God given right for the United States to stretch from the Atlantic Ocean to the Pacific. He called it "Manifest Destiny". Taylor shared in this belief. However there were three major obstacles to reaching this goal. The two most formidable were the huge Mexican States; Alta California that lay along the Pacific for hundreds of miles, and Nueva

Mejico that lay adjoining Texas. The third obstacle was the Oregon Territory that lay north of Alta California along the Pacific. The British and Americans were in heated argument about which country would have control of that large tract of land.

As President Polk had spoken, it became obvious to Taylor that the man had decided upon a strategy to wrest control of those large land areas from their present owners. To obtain the Mexican land, Polk had sent an emissary John Slidell to Mexico City with an offer to buy Nueva Mejico for $3,000,000 and Alta California for $2,500,000. Taylor knew a proud nation would never sell half of its land, not for any amount of money. Polk also knew that. The offer was but a ruse to allow Slidell to visit the Mexican Capitol and discover what he could about the Mexican readiness for battle.

Slidell had discovered the Mexican army consisted of approximately twenty thousand men, with the major portion stationed at Matamoros and Monterrey in the northern part of the nation to resist any invasion by the Americans. Most of the remainder was stationed at Vera Cruz on the south coast and Mexico City in the center of the nation.

Polk, learning the Mexican land could not be bought, had but one option, take it from them by force. Taylor knew he had been chosen to play a large part in putting the plan into action due to his success in the Blackhawk War in the west and the more recent war with the Seminoles in Florida.

Polk had directed Taylor to assemble an army upon land near Corpus Christi, land claimed by both Texas and Mexico, and await his orders. Over the following months, Taylor had drawn men from the forts in the west and from the military bases in the east, adding to three thousand and four hundred men. New recruits had now brought his number of troopers to its present size. Training in the use of weapons; muskets, bayonets, and cannon, and practice in maneuvering various size army units had been continuous eight hours a day since January. He believed his small army was ready for a fight.

Taylor had now received orders to march his army south to the Rio Grande. The word "provoke" was not mentioned in the orders. Still, Taylor knew his task was to take some action to cause the Mexicans to attack the Americans and start a war. He was then to defeat the Mexican army in battle and force the government to surrender Nuevo Mejico and Alta California. With the Mexican troops outnumbering him at more than four to one and fighting on their own land, defeating them would be a daunting task. Due to that, he must always be the aggressor so that he could attack and defeat the Mexican Army piecemeal and at a time and place of his choosing.

"General Taylor, Worth reporting," a man called from the entrance to the tent.

"Come in, general."

Worth entered and saluted. Taylor gestured at the second chair in the tent.

"Be seated."

As Worth seated himself, his eyes fell upon the mail pouch on the desk. An expression of understanding of its meaning washed over his face.

"You're correct," Taylor said and allowed himself a brief smile. "It's time we moved south and I'm informing President Polk and Secretary Marcy that we are doing that."

Worth nodded. "The men are well trained and ready, sir."

"I agree. Now as to our plan. First we will keep five hundred men here at Fort Polk to guard our supply base."

"It'll be a hard march," Worth said. "Water will be scarce as we move ever farther south. And feed for the animals too."

Taylor nodded agreement. "I agree, so we'll move our force in three contingents a day apart."

Taylor took up a sheet of paper. "Let's get the plan down in writing so there are no mistakes in how we position the troopers, dragoons, weapons, and supplies for the march."

***

General Taylor, dressed in full uniform, rode into Corpus Christi astride his personal horse "Old Whitey". Four Dragoons armed with pistols and sabers and mounted on four matching black horses, rode close behind. Taylor thought that he and the Dragoons made a splendid show. He led onward along the main street that led to the waterfront where the mail packet was anchored.

Taylor liked the hustle and bustle, the activity of the little town; the buggies with neatly clothed people, men on horseback and the stores on the plaza with their doors invitingly open. He much enjoyed the varied colors of the buildings, many painted white, others brown of several shades, a few dark blue or red, one of green, the color of young clover. The town's location on the coast with its shipping made for a thriving town. The presence of the American army and its need for supplies had added to its business.

He studied the people on the street and on the sidewalks, about an even mixture of Americans and Mexicans, he judged. The Americans watched with friendly interest, some nodded, some lifted a hand. The Mexicans stared with solemn, glum faces. A group of several young Mexican man stared at him with open hostility. This had been a Mexican town until the Texans under Sam Houston had beaten General Santa Ana in battle and he had surrendered the land more than a decade earlier. The anger of that defeat still lay in the hearts of the Mexicans. Taylor with his army would soon add to their anger.

Closer to the waterfront, Taylor passed a blacksmith shop with its wide double doors standing open to allow the slow breeze to carry away the heat from the forge. The entire interior was in view, the smoking forge, two workbenches and two anvils.

A tall, blond headed young blacksmith, wearing a leather apron that covered his front from chest down to his knees, came and stood in front of the smithy. He scooped sweat from his forehead with a curved finger and flicked the brine onto the ground. His eyes locked with Taylor's eyes,

At that flick of sweat, Taylor called out to the blacksmith. "Why not stop hammering hot iron and join the army?"

The blacksmith considered that for three seconds. "I just might do that," he called back in a strong voice.

Taylor touched his hat to the smithy and rode onward.

A short distance later, Taylor came within sight of the Gulf of Mexico and found its water blue and with but the smallest of waves and stretching as far as he could see. He smiled at the beauty of the water and rode on to the waterfront with its two short docks. A man sat on the nearer dock and worked at mending fishing net. A boy of six or seven fished with a pole and line close by the man's side. Taylor thought the boy might be the grandson of the man. Taylor felt a pang of regret that he was not sitting by some quiet water and fishing with one or more of his grandsons. Soon, he thought, soon now.

Taylor spoke to the man. "How much to row me out to that ship? He pointed at the mail packet anchored some forty yards off shore due to the water being too shallow to come closer. Cargo and passengers were transported to shore by large, flat bottomed rowboats propelled by oarsmen.

"A quarter would do it," replied the man.

"And wait to bring me back. Not Long."

The man nodded.

Taylor dismounted and handed the reins of Old Whitey to the nearest dragoon. He removed his mail pouch from a saddle bag and climbed into the rowboat.

"Don't fall in," the man called to the boy, who smiled and nodded.

Taylor evaluated the ship as they approached. She was a sleek, sharp bowed clipper ship painted black with three tall masts, each of which held six yard arms with tan colored canvas sails pulled up tightly to them and tied there. Lettering in white painted on the side of the ship near the bow, proclaimed her to be the Two Brothers of the Cunard Line. Taylor judged she would be fast.

The man on the oars brought the rowboat up against the gangway hanging over the side. Taylor climbed out of the rowboat and up the gangway to the deck of the ship.

The seaman on deck saluted him. "Welcome aboard, General Taylor."

"Is the captain aboard?" Taylor said.

"Yes, sir, in his cabin," replied the seaman and turned to a cabin boy of twelve or so. "Peter, tell the captain that General Taylor is aboard."

The boy bobbed his head and dashed away on flying feet.

A moment later the captain, a tall, angular man, dressed in a blue naval uniform, came striding along the deck.

"Good to see you General Taylor."

"And you too, Captain Smithson."

"I was about to send a messenger out to your camp to see if you had any mail to go. And I see that you do. Come along to the mail room and we'll stow it away."

Taylor followed Smithson along the deck and into the mail room located amidships. There the captain unlocked an iron safe bolted to the deck. Lettering on its side declared it to be U. S. Mail. Taylor placed his pouch within it.

"Safe and sound," said the captain as he relocked the safe.

"Thank you, captain. It must be delivered directly to the president."

"I shall take care of that personally."

"How long before you reach Washington?"

"Two Brothers is a fast ship. Still it will take eight days to reach New Orleans where I must pick up mail and passengers and then another fifteen days to reach Washington. That's if the winds are favorable."

Taylor nodded his understanding. President Polk would not know the contents of his report for those twenty three days. By that time, Taylor would have fought battles with the Mexicans and been victorious, or disastrously defeated. He could be dead.

"Will you have a drink with me?"

"Thanks, captain, but no. The next time we meet."

Smithson frowned with disappointment. Taylor made a small smile at the man's expression. Smithson did indeed like a reason for having a drink.

Taylor left the ship and was rowed to the dock. He paid the money owed, mounted Old Whitey and rode toward the recruiting office he had established on the town square.

Chapter Two

Butterfly Moon, September, 1846
Monterrey, Northern Mexico

Young Charlie Bell came to consciousness bit by bit with a horrible headache and a loud roaring in his ears. Where was he? What had happened? He couldn't recall. He opened his eyes to total darkness. He felt the strange sensation that he was floating in a pit with its walls close about him. He tried to reach out to feel the walls to test whether or not he truly was in a pit, but his arms refused to move. He was paralyzed. His heart was suddenly hammering against his ribs.

He stared hard into the blackness left and right, straining to make out some form that would tell him about his surroundings. He saw nothing. He looked upward and again saw nothing. Then far above him and barely discernible a tiny glimmer of light came into focus. By some means that Charlie did not understand, he knew that the light was life itself and that he must reach it. Should he fail, he would die.

He wanted to live! God! How he wanted to live! He focused his will, concentrating his every thought on rising through the darkness to the light. He remained stationary with that same sensation of floating. UP! Up! Charlie shouted out in a thunderous, silent cry.

Slowly he began to rise, but, oh, so slowly, so very slowly. The spot of light grew gradually larger, increasing from the size of a dime to a silver dollar, and then larger still. He came to full consciousness to find himself lying on stony ground and with the side of his face and blond head in a pool of blood. His head ached terribly, as if his skull had been split open and poured full of molten iron. He sensed danger all around him and he lay perfectly still and fought to gather his scrambled senses.

Again the questions came. What had happened? Where was he? He struggled with that question. Then the memory of how he came to be in this place and hurting so terribly came rushing back.

Charlie had killed two Mexican soldiers with musket balls and one with his bayonet and was in a bayonet fight with a fourth Mexican, a young and very quick soldier. The fellow fought bravely and fiercely. Still, Charlie had the advantage for he was nearly a foot taller than the Mexican and his arms were longer and his reach with the bayonet much greater. He had the man on the defensive and was ready to burst past his defense and make a final, killing stab into his body with the bayonet.

As that thought of victory over his opponent came to Charlie, he caught a glimpse in the sky close above of a swiftly moving cannonball arching down from the heavens, its path toward the Mexican soldier and himself marked by a trail of gray-white smoke from its burning fuse. Before Charlie could act, the cannonball landed close by and the burning fuse carried its fire inside and ignited the gunpowder within.

The explosion, a brilliant red and orange flash, sent the 90 lead balls embedded inside the cannonball, the hundreds of sharp iron shrapnel of the shattered shell of the cannonball itself, spewing out in a great rain of death. Charlie felt a hellish blow on his head and the world went black.

How long had he lain unconscious from that explosion? It must have been hours for the blood on the ground was congealed and dark and he was God awfully thirsty. He felt a sudden chill. Who had won the battle? Would he soon be a prisoner of the Mexicans? That could bring immediate execution.

He listened for a sound, any sound that would tell him that other soldiers, enemy or comrades, were alive somewhere close by. There was only silence, as if all living things had been killed, or had become frightened by the deadly fighting and had hidden away in some secret place.

Charlie warily raised his head to look about to see what danger there might be, what damage the cannonball had done to the other soldiers on the ground. The young Mexican he had been fighting lay on his back a body length distant from Charlie. He did not move. Further away were nearly a score of broken, bleeding bodies, both American and Mexican soldiers alike, broken into contorted, grotesque positions by the explosion. One man was missing his head, only the bloody stump of his neck remained. The body of another man had been blown against the trunk of a large tree, his arms were extended and wrapped around the tree, as if embracing a lover. Another Mexican was smashed against a boulder. Charlie shivered at the death so close about him. A Mexican artilleryman had made a terrible miscalculation in aiming his cannon and had dropped a cannonball, not only upon Americans, but also upon his own comrades.

Charlie lifted a hand to examine the wound on his aching head. His searching fingers found a section of his scalp half as big as his hand had been torn from the left side of his skull and the bloody flap of skin and hair hung down past his ear.

Anger surged through him. Why hadn't the men who drove the ambulance wagons found him and carried him to the hospital so that the surgeons could sew him back together? Or had they made their search and failed to find him? He shoved the anger away. He must not depend on someone to save him. He would rest and gather enough strength to somehow get himself to the hospital. His anger increased. Why the hell had he joined the army and come to this foreign land to fight a war?

Charlie's journey had begun in Corpus Christi, Texas where he lived with his father in a tiny, one bedroom house near the waterfront. His mother had died of typhoid fever when he was but a toddler. His father worked on the docks as a longshoreman loading and unloading the ships that journeyed to distant ports of the world. When Charlie became fourteen years old, his father left, signing on as a crewman on a ship bound for London. He left Charlie, a skinny, blond headed, blue eyed boy, behind as an apprentice to the blacksmith Harold Ayers who owned a smithy in the town. Charlie's pay for his work was fifty cents a week and a cot to sleep on in a small room at the rear of the smithy.

Ayers was fifty two years old and a confirmed bachelor. He lived in an apartment above the smithy. He was known as a skilled craftsman, and somewhat of a rascal who liked his whiskey and women. Charlie was to learn more about this side of Ayers.

Ayers spoke fluent Spanish and due to that ability, many of his customers were Mexican. He told Charlie that he must quickly learn the language so that he too could communicate with the men who brought things to be repaired, and especially to understand the descriptions of items they desired to be made. Ayers had smiled an added, "Another good reason to learn Spanish is that half of the pretty girls in Corpus Christi speak only Spanish."

Charlie wanted to learn and he became an attentive pupil as Ayers taught him while they worked, or setting together and resting, or in the evenings after the last meal of the day.

Charlie was tall for his age, and during the following months working for Ayers, he continued to grow rapidly, and he gained solid muscle from lifting heavy pieces of iron and swinging a hammer thousands of times each day to bend and shape red hot metal into tools and other items requested by customers. Ayers also received orders to create items with very close adherence to dimensions. He had tools for creating replacement parts for broken instruments and tools used in all manner of trades. Making parts for firearms was Charlie's favorite task. After finishing repairs on a gun, Ayers and he would take it into the country and test it by firing at targets. Under Ayers's guidance, he became a skilled marksman with both pistol and rifle.

As Charlie matured, he began to wonder about Ayers's Saturday trips into west Corpus Christi. Sometimes the man carried home bruises from fights. Then one day as they worked, he gathered courage and asked Ayers why he went into Corpus Christi so often.

Ayers had ceased work and studied Charlie for a few seconds. Then he grinned. "Yeah, you'er big enough to know the facts of life."

"I know the facts of life," Charlie retorted.

"Then you know all about girls?"

"I know about girls."

"How about full grown women? How about loose women?"

"What do you mean loose women?"

"Those that like to make love. Oh, sometimes they may charge a little. But most times they do it for free."

Ayers grinned at Charlie. "When you turn eighteen, I'll introduce you to some pretty ones. How about that?"

Charlie, a little embarrassed, turned to his work and said nothing.

He did not like being a blacksmith with the constant smell of burning charcoal and breathing the lung burning smoke that sometimes was so dense he could taste it, and the incessant clang of Ayres's and his hammer beating upon metal made his ears ache.

He shoved the scythe blade that he was making into the red hot charcoal and stepped to the open door to allow the ocean breeze to cool him.

On the street, an army officer dressed in uniform and mounted on a fine white horse was passing. Four mounted Dragoons followed close behind as escort. The officer had called out to Charlie to stop pounding hot iron and join the army. That was indeed a tempting thought. The Corpus Christi newspaper was full of the news about the growing threat of war between Mexico and the United States over millions of acres of land both claimed along the Rio Grande. The newspaper also carried notices of the army seeking recruits.

Charlie, now sixteen, lied about his age, telling the recruitment officer that he was eighteen and signed the enlistment papers for a two year hitch in the army. The pay would be eight dollars a month. He was issued a blue wool uniform, a .69 caliber musket with cartridge box, a blanket, and a haversack for his army issue of items and a very scant number of personal belongings. He was assigned to the 5th Infantry Regiment of the army under the command of Captain Evan McIntosh.

March 8, two days after Charlie's enlistment, General Taylor, mounted upon his white horse, led his army of 3,500 men out of their quarters at Fort Polk and southwest into the wilderness toward the Rio Grande. A company of 400 Dragoons, riding four abreast with their horses blowing and snorting and saddle leather creaking, led the way. Following the Dragoons was a unit of "Flying Artillery" with their 4-pound bronze cannon, so called due to the iron balls they fired weighing that amount, slung low between iron rimmed wheels and pulled by a team of horses. Charlie's 5th Infantry followed the artillery and led the remaining four infantry units. Behind the infantry rolled the heavy cannon, big 18-pounders and 8-pounders. Charlie thought the men and their weapons were a grand sight.

Spring like weather gave away to cloudless, burning days as Charlie marched with the army south across the sun-baked plains. He was traveling as lightly as possible, still, with his army nine-and-a half pound musket, several rounds of ammunition, a bayonet, a canteen of water, a haversack which contained a blanket, food rations, and a few personal items, he was carrying thirty pounds, or a bit more. After a day of marching, that load seemed to have doubled in weight.

He had observed men laboring under their loads. The small trooper marching by his side had obvious difficulty carrying his. Charlie had reached out to relieve him of his musket, but had caught himself, concerned the fellow would be offended, that he was not man enough to carry his own gear.

Adding to Charlie's misery, the blue woolen uniform, designed for use in cooler northern climes, was suffocating and hc wanted to rip if off. His cap with its short bill gave little protection from the sun and his face and the back of his neck burned and blistered, cracked and ran. Further, the pound of the iron shod hooves of the horses and the iron rimmed wheels of the cannon ahead of Charlie had crushed the earth into deep dust which made each step difficult. Worse yet, the water holes were small and far apart and the men and horses were often thirsty. Then the open plain gave way to thorny bushes, cactus and chaparral and the march became even harsher. The grumble and complaints of the troopers grew louder.

Charlie, resting sweaty and weary in the evenings, recalled the days with Ayers at the smithy. After a hard day's work, Ayers and he would walk the short distance to the shore of the Gulf, strip off their clothing and wash it, wring it free of as much water as possible, and allow it to dry hanging on drift wood while they dove and swam in the clean blue water. Charlie knew those pleasant times would never happen again.

General Taylor, mounted upon his white horse, rode up and down the two miles long line of moving men, weapons and wagons twice each day, mid-morning and mid-afternoon checking everyone and everything's condition. He gave no sign he recognized Charlie among the trudging troopers. That bothered Charlie a little.

Charlie understood why a general would ride horse-back, but he envied the other officers riding easily upon their horses while he and the ordinary troopers labored so strenuously. He saw no compassion on their faces. Perhaps they expected to ride due to their station. Could it be that one common soldier had little value to them? Perhaps it required a squad, or maybe an entire platoon to acquire value. Did other men have these same thoughts? Charlie did not like the direction his thoughts were taking and pulled them away.

***

Twenty days after leaving Corpus Christi, Charlie stood with his comrades and stared across the one hundred yards wide and waist deep Rio Grande at the aged Mexican city of Matamoros. He thought it a fairy city with its stone and adobe buildings, most of them painted white, and the large number of green plants and large trees. There seem to him to be an excess number of churches; he could identify them by their size and the tall steeples.

Men, women and children had climbed to the roof tops of the buildings lining the river to look at the American troops. Half a score of pretty young women came out of the town and down to the water. They talked among themselves, and then laughing, took off their clothes and waded into the slow current of water and bathed. The Americans called out good naturedly to the women.

A few young American officers rode their horses into the water until the animals were belly deep. They held out there arms to the dusky skinned girls and motioned for them to come. They girls laughed and splashed water in the direction of the Americans but did not cross the river.

Charlie had never seen a naked girl, and he gave their slender young bodies close scrutiny. They were obviously enjoying showing themselves to the hundreds of Americans, seemingly unafraid as if the broad sheet of river water would keep them safe. As they splashed about, they waved at the Americans and smiled mischievously with their black eyes flashing teasing glances at them. To Charlie, their voices, especially their laughter, had a pleasant musical sound. He again and again traced the contours of the girls' naked bodies, lingering over the sight of their bare breast and rounded hips. There is mystery and beauty in girls, he thought. He was stimulated mightily and in a most enjoyable way.

A Mexican Army Captain, his uniform very similar in color to the American uniform, arrived on horseback at the river's edge. He stared across the water at the Americans for a moment, then turned to the girls and ordered them out of the water.

Still laughing, the girls waded out of the water, picked up their clothing and dressed. Casting looks back over their shoulder at the Americans, they walked away toward the town.

The army captain shouted out angrily across the river to the Americans that they were on Mexican territory and they must leave.

Charlie understood the Mexican officer and turned to see what the American officers would do. They ignored the officer. Charlie wondered how many of them understood Spanish. Not many he guessed.

General Taylor also ignored the Mexican officer's words. He ordered his small army into bivouac on a flat, grassy area seven miles north of Matamoros. The Americans raised an American flag on a thirty foot tall pole and waited for the Mexicans to start the fighting.

***

On May 8, Charlie's infantry company was called to assemble. The Mexican Army had crossed to the north side of the Rio Grande and General Taylor was marching his men out to meet them. Charlie sweated as he hurried with his company south to meet the enemy, and he worried. What exactly was expected of him? Would he and his comrades just simply be thrown at the Mexicans and fight as best they could? Or did General Taylor have a plan.

They came into sight of the Mexicans arranged for battle on the south side of a place named Palo Alto, Tall Trees in Spanish, a plain two miles wide and covered with stiff, sharply pointed grass standing chest high. Tall trees covered two small hills on the left and right side gave the plain its name. Behind the Mexicans were dense thickets of chaparral. The Mexican line of soldiers was a mile long with a company of Lancers anchoring each end. Their many bronze cannons glisten in the bright sunlight.

The Americans formed up behind their batteries of cannons half a mile distant and waited for the Mexicans to start the battle.

In the early afternoon, the Mexicans opened fire with their 4-pound and 8-pound cannons upon the Americans. To Charlie's surprise, some of the projectiles fell short. Upon striking the ground, the round balls ricocheted onward but so slowly that they could be seen coming by the movement of the grass and the Americans could jump aside to let them pass harmlessly by.

The Americans fired their primed 8-pound and 18-pound cannon loaded with either solid iron balls or round canisters filled with metal shards that exploded in midair and spread the deadly projectiles like a shotgun over large areas. Charlie could see gaping holes suddenly appear in the Mexican line.

Captain McIntosh's voice boomed out. "Fifth Infantry! Form square! Form square"

Charlie hurriedly took his place in the square of troopers, a tactical shape long used by infantry to withstand a cavalry charge. Horses would resist striking a wall of men standing shoulder to shoulder and muskets with bayonets extended.

He flung a look across the plain to see what had caused the call to form the square. A company of Mexican Cavalry, called Lancers due to the nine feet long lances they used for fighting, had broken from the chaparral on the left end of the Mexican line and was racing toward the 5th Infantry. He thought the charging Lancers in their blue uniforms and their red banners whipping in the wind were a grand sight. The Lancers lowered their lances to strike.

"Stand ready to fire," shouted McIntosh.

The square of troopers raised their muskets with bayonets attached. The Lancers were positioned to strike Charlie's side of the square and the one to his right. He aimed his musket at the chest of a man in the center of the line of Lancers.

"Fire," shouted McIntosh.

Charlie fired, the strong recoil of the musket unfelt. He saw the Lancer jerk backward as the lead ball struck his chest. The man clutched at the saddle horn and struggled to remain on his mount. His legs came loose from their grip on the horse and he rolled from the saddle. He fell face down into the tall grass and vanished from view.

Charlie caught a breath that his intense concentration had stopped. He had killed his first man, a man he did not hate, did not even know. He knew the image of the Lancer's reaction to the deadly bullet would be forever embedded in his memory.

The Lancers, slowed by the boggy ground and tall grass and peppered with musket balls, drew up forty yards short of the American square. They had taken heavy losses, men falling from saddles, and horses, wounded by miss-aimed American bullets, screaming out in wild animal pain.

"Reload," shouted McIntosh.

Charlie dropped the butt of his musket onto the ground, flipped open his cartridge box, pulled out a packet of gunpowder, tore it open with his teeth, poured the contents down the barrel of the gun, stuck the cloth into the end of the barrel, dug a lead ball from the box, placed it on the wadding and shoved both into the end of the barrel with a thumb, jerked the wooden ramrod from its slot under the barrel, inserted it into the barrel and rammed the wadding and ball down firmly against the gunpowder. He replaced the rod under the barrel, swiftly fished a primer cap from the box and pressed it down over the firing nipple.

Charlie hurriedly looked at the Lancers where their captain was riding among his milling horsemen and striking them with the flat of his saber, and shouting for them to form up for a charge. They began to form a line, reining their mounts to face the Americans and aiming the sharp iron points of their lances ahead.

Captain McIntosh, seeing Charlie had reloaded and ready to shoot, spurred his horse close.

"Shoot that officer!" McIntosh commanded and stabbed a hand at the Lancer Captain.

Charlie raised his musket and fired. The bullet struck true to his point of aim and knocked the officer from his saddle.

Seeing their officer dead, the remaining Lancers milled about for a moment, then they broke and as one body, reined their mounts swiftly around, kicked them in the ribs and fled out of range of the American muskets, and onward toward their lines, leaving their wounded and dead lying hidden in the tall grass.

Charlie shivered and drew a trembling breath of air. He had killed two men, saw them flinch as his bullets struck and tumble from their mounts. So easy to kill, so awful to have done it.

Charlie stood and only half seeing the battlefield as the Mexicans again fired their cannon. They had increased the powder charges of their cannon and were striking the Americans. The Americans returned an even heavier fire.

A burning wad from one of the Mexican cannon fell into the grass and set it on fire with red and orange flames leaping. The fire quickly spread with smoke forming and growing into a thick cloud that blanketed the battlefield. With each enemy hid from the other, the cannon fire ceased.

The sun fell to lay on the far horizon before the fire had burned itself out. With the smoke thinning and drifting away with the wind, the Mexicans could be seen breaking formation and moving away to the south toward the Rio Grande, leaving their dead and wounded laying on the battleground.

McIntosh called out, "Fall out and rest. If you need water, there's a pond just over there." He pointed.

Charlie sat down on the ground in the area where the boots of the troopers of the square had smashed down the grass. He drank from his canteen, the stale, warm water sweet in his parched mouth.

In the early darkness of the night, the American hospital wagons came, and using the frail light cast by the feeble lights of oil lanterns, gathered up the wounded. The dead would have to wait until daylight.

Charlie and his comrades ate rations from their packs and lay down to rest on their blankets. Now and again during the black night, Charlie heard the cry for help from the wounded Mexicans. None was given by the Americans.

***

At first light of the day after the battle, Charlie rose from where he slept in the grass of Palo Alto and marched out with his regiment in pursuit of the enemy south through rolling hills covered with a thick stand of trees and tangled chaparral. Five miles onward they were fired upon by Mexican cannon entrenched at Resaca de la Palma, a dry river bed, an old, abandoned meander of the Rio Grande. The channel was two miles long and two hundred feet wide and deep to twice the height of a man. Both banks were heavily forested with trees and thickets of chaparral.

General Taylor ordered Charlie's 5th Infantry to make the direct frontal attack to silence the cannon. A company of Dragoons was ordered to circle in behind the cannons and attack from the rear.

Charlie and his comrades hurried forward. Immediately upon entering the trees and thick chaparral, his company was forced to break into squads to move onward. In but a few yards more, the chaparral was even denser and tangled and the squads divided into groups of three or four men blundering onward and unable to see but a few feet ahead. They found the enemy and the fighting began, furious and disorganized, enemies materializing out of the chaparral, musket shots up close, bloody hand-to-hand with bayonets, musket butts. Charlie fought and slew men trying to kill him. A strongly built, heavily bearded Mexican gave him a wound across the ribs with a bayonet before Charlie could bayonet him to death.

Charlie and his regiment reached the top of the bank of the dry river channel and ran into heavy musket fire from the Mexicans guarding five 6-pound cannons. The Americans returned the fire and killing many and routing the remainder that fled south toward the Rio Grande. The Americans rushed after the swiftly fleeing enemy.

Charlie, breathing hard and sweating from a three miles chase, reached the Rio Grande and stopped on the top of the river bank. Many Mexican soldiers had thrown away their weapons and plunged into the water and swam to the far side to escape. Some could not swim and were flailing helplessly at the water. Others were sinking and not resurfacing. Several scores were huddled together, penned between the Americans and the water. Charlie looked beyond the river where hundreds of men in blue uniforms were fleeing south.

Charlie, hurting from his wound and many jabs and scratches from the sharp thorns of the chaparral, leaned against a tree and waited for orders. He was glad when the word came down from General Taylor not to pursue the fleeing Mexicans. Instead, the general directed camp to be set up to allow time for the men to rest, the wounded to be found and treated, the dead buried.

A day later and his wounds treated, Charlie's with his 5th Infantry forded the Rio Grande, and with wet feet and not one Mexican soldier in sight, entered Matamoros.

General Taylor put the city under martial law.

***

In mid-August, Charlie's 5th Infantry was again on the move as General Taylor, his army now reinforced to six thousand men by arrival of new recruits, led south toward the 250 year old fortress city of Monterrey, the largest city in northern Mexico. On the eighteenth of the month after a hot, strenuous march, the Americans reached the plains just north of Monterrey. By late in the day, the Americans had set up their encampment.

With work finished, Charlie, along with several others of his squad, climbed to the top of a close by hill from which they could study the city. A chill ran along his spine as he gazed at the great wall that protected the city, and close by lay Fort El Diablo with its tall, stone ramparts with cannons showing, and the many cannons visible on the two fortified hills that overlooked the city. Many men would die in capturing Monterrey.

For two days, General Taylor and his senior officers rode around the walled city and examining its fortifications. On the morning of the third day, September 20, he ordered a three pronged attack upon the city. Charlie's 5th Infantry was ordered to capture Fort El Diablo with its many cannons and Mexican soldiers. On the morning of the second day of that deadly fight for the fort, the wrongly aimed cannon ball had landed and exploded and Charlie had lost consciousness.

A sound broke through Charlie's remembrances of how he came to be lying in his own blood and he jerked back to the here and now awareness of his surroundings. The sound came again and he recognized the thud of horse hooves and the rattle of trace chains and grind of iron rimmed wheels of a wagon on the stony ground.

"Whoa," called a man and the sounds ceased.

Charlie turned his aching head to look. His heart gave a sudden surge for the sound had been made by an

American hospital ambulance. The vehicle was a flat-bed wagon with six inch sideboards. The wooden body of the wagon was painted blue, the iron rimmed wheels, with their strong oak spokes, were painted a dark brown. A team of gray horses pulled the ambulance.

Two large Americans in the blue uniforms of the American army sat on the seat of the wagon. The red arm bands tied over their upper arms told that they were hospital orderlies.

"Goddamn, Ross, look what a cannonball did to those poor bastards," the larger man said.

"Sure did mangle them," Ross replied.

Ross's eyes halted their sweep of the area and fixed on Charlie. "One of our boys is still alive."

"I don't see how the hell he could be for that cannon ball landed on top of him."

"Let's get him loaded quick and back to camp," said Ross.

The second man stabbed a finger at the black clouds gathering over the hills close by to the north. "Those damn clouds are getting ready to pour."

The men jumped down from the wagon and hurried to Charlie and knelt beside him.

"Looks like you're still in the land of the livin'," Ross said.

"Must be for I hurt like hell," Charlie replied weakly.

"You got cause for your scalp is half peeled from your skull."

"Did we win?" Charlie said.

"Yeah. But it took two days to get over the wall," Ross said.

"And we had a lot of boys killed and hurt doing it," said the second man.

"Let's stop jabbering and get him loaded," said Ross.

Charlie felt strong hands catch him by the legs and shoulders. A moment later he was placed on the blanket padded bed of the wagon where several other wounded soldiers lay.

"Did you see that?" Ross said.

"See what?" said the big man.

"That little Mex over there's alive. He should've called out."

"He probably thinks we're going to kill him."

"Looks like he's almost lost a leg."

"Well, we've got orders to bring Mexs to the hospital same as our own fellows. Let's get him loaded."

A few seconds later the Mexican was placed beside Charlie in the wagon. He looked into the face of the man only a few inches way. The brown face was smeared with dirt and a sliver of shrapnel protruded half an inch from a cheek bone. Blood had flowed from around the metal and hardened into a large scab.

Charlie jerked with recognition. The face was that of the young Mexican that had been trying to kill him with his bayonet when the cannonball exploded. Charlie smile grimly at the strangeness of seeing his enemy up so close, and both of them seriously wounded.

The Mexican gave him a hate filled stare and turned away.

"Damn, it's starting to rain and we've got half a mile to go," said Ross. "Lay the whip to those nags."

A whip cracked and the wagon moved, bouncing and careening over the rough, rocky ground. Several of the wounded soldiers cried out with the added pain caused by the jarring and shaking. One shouted curses at the driver. He ignored the men's complaints, called out to his horses and popped his whip over their heads to hurry them onward.

The bottom of the black clouds split open and a torrent of cold water poured down upon the men, the huge drops striking like hail and drenching them to the skin. Charlie began to shiver. He made no sound for what was the good of that.

Minutes later the wagon pulled to a stop at the open front of a huge hospital tent sagging under the downpour of rain and shedding water in sheets. Several orderlies with stretchers rushed into the rain and hastily loaded the wounded men and hustled them into the tent.

Moving his head gently, Charlie looked about the tent and saw at least a half dozen operating tables where surgeons with blood spattered aprons were cutting flesh with sharp scalpels, bone with saws, and sewing torn flesh back together with needle and thread; with the surgeons calling out crisp orders to the husky orderlies to hold the wounded soldier motionless while the operation was performed. With no pain killers, wounded men groaned and cried out from the great suffering. At half a dozen other tables, orderlies were hurriedly wiping away the blood and pieces of flesh and bone from the last operation. Several arms and legs were piled near the rear exit of the tent. Charlie felt a great sadness. The battle had been costly in human suffering, and human bodies.

The orderlies carrying Charlie halted at an empty operating table. The two large assistants of the surgeon lifted him off the stretcher and onto the table.

"Hold him down tightly," the surgeon, a tall, thin man, directed his two assistants.

Strong hands caught Charlie by the shoulders and pressed him down against the table. A second pair of big hands clamped his head in a vise-like hold just below the hairline.

"Don't move, soldier," said the surgeon. "I'm going to check your wound."

The surgeon, using a soft cloth and soapy water from a pan, began to wash the dirt and blood from Charlie's scalp and from the flap of skin and hair.

Finishing the task, he spoke, "You're damn lucky. A fraction of an inch closer and whatever hit you would have cracked your skull. As it is, all you have is a groove in the bone. I can cover that with your scalp. But you'll always have a visible part in your hair."

Charlie did not feel lucky. He steeled himself against the pain and did not cry out as the surgeon stretched and shaped the flap of skin and hair back to its original shape, as near as possible, and began sewing with the needle and thread.

As the surgeon worked, Charlie made a profound decision and that helped him through the pain filled minutes under the surgeon's hands. He was but sixteen and had fought in three battles and had shot or bayoneted several men to death. He was finished with war and killing.

Chapter Three

On the morning of the fourth day of Charlie's stay in the hospital tent, he sat on his cot and waited for the surgeon, who was making his morning visit of the wounded, to get to him. A score of other men also silently waited sitting or lying on their beds. The surgeon was accompanied by a hospital orderly carrying a large wooden tray containing the various items that might be needed to treat the injuries. The pungent odor of freshly applied salves and ointments was heavy on the air.

The surgeon, the same tall thin man who had operated on Charlie, was very methodical and thorough as he removed the blood stained bandages of each man, inspected the injury and covered it with a fresh white bandage. He always took a moment to say a few words to the man about the condition of his wound.

The surgeon came to Charlie and examined his wound. "Soldier, your wound is healing without a sign of infection. And the scar won't be all that noticeable."

"How about my headaches, sir?" Charlie asked. "They're pretty bad."

"How often do you have them?"

"Several every day, and I haven't been getting much sleep these past days because of them."

"Head wounds are the toughest kind of wounds to predict. The outside can heal but the damage done to the brain being jarred and slammed against the skull is unknown. However, by having seen several wounds such as yours during the past several weeks, my best guess is that your headaches will gradually go away. But there's no guarantee of that."

The surgeon moved away to the wounded man on the next cot. The hospital orderly followed closely behind with the tray of medicines and bandages.

Charlie lay down on the cot and shut his eyes. He tried to ignore his throbbing headache.

His thoughts turned to the fighting of the last battle. The image of the face of the small Mexican soldier that had fought him so bravely had frequently appeared before him. He remembered plainly every feature of the young, brown face that had lain so close to his own in the hospital wagon. He remembered the hate-filled look the man had given him. He also remembered the cold rain that had fallen upon both of them, making no distinction between the Mexican and the American, two foolish men that had tried to kill each other. Now, for some reason he could not identify, he felt a great need to see if the man still lived? Charlie knew that he wanted the man to be alive. If he was, he would be in one of the hospital tents.

***

Charlie awoke in the late-afternoon with his headache somewhat lessened and a mission to accomplish. The surgeon had not said that he must remain in the hospital tent, so he rose from the cot, took up the hated wool uniform from where it hung on the head of his cot, dressed, pulled on his boots and left the hospital.

He paused to look out over the half mile square tent encampment of the army. The hospital tents, nearly a score of them, were on the highest ground near the center of the encampment so that they would catch the most cooling breezes. Part of the tents held men wounded in battle, others the sick from diseases, mostly dysentery and typhoid fever. The wounded were not mixed with the ill.

Not far from the hospital were the kitchen tents and the mess tents where the soldiers ate. The tents of the officers, along with Taylor's and his aids, were off by themselves on the far right side of the encampment. The hundreds of tents for the common soldier were in a broad field on the opposite side of the encampment. Beyond those were the cannons drawn up in neat rows and the pastures for the horses of the cavalry, the officers' mounts and the many draft horses used for pulling the cannon and the scores of wagons transporting the army's supplies. Charlie could make out sentries moving on their assigned patrols around the perimeter of the camp.

He walked toward the hospital tent where a trooper with a musket stood guard. That would be the hospital for the wounded Mexicans.

As he drew close, he spoke to the guard. "I want to see one of the prisoners. That ok?"

"Why?" asked the guard with surprise.

"I want to see if he's still alive. He was fighting me when the cannonball hit us." Charlie touched the bandage on his head.

The guard gave that a few seconds of thought. "I guess that'd be okay." He stepped aside.

Charlie entered the tent and cast a look around at the rows of cots all crowded close together and holding at least half a hundred wounded Mexican soldiers. At first, he did not see the man he sought. Then to his relief, he caught sight of him lying motionlessly and covered by a sheet, except for the lower half of his right leg that was wrapped in a bandage.

Charlie drew close to the cot and looked down at the small, brown skinned, black haired fellow lying with his eyes closed. So still did he lie, so pinched and drawn was his face with the bones showed starkly, Charlie though him dead.

The Mexican's eyes opened, and falling upon Charlie, flashed sharp alarm. He flinched back and his hands shot up to fend Charlie off.

"Hello," Charlie said in Spanish and with a friendly tone. The action of the man saddened him.

"Go away," said the Mexican, his voice savage and his black eyes full of hate. He turned his face away.

Charlie looked down at the fellow for a few seconds, then turned and left the hospital tent.

A few minutes later as Charlie re-entered his hospital tent, the surgeon was present and saw him. He called out, "Private Bell, since you're well enough to go wandering about, I'll release you to return to your outfit. Your bed is needed by others. You will be on light duty, no drilling or any strenuous activity. Report here each morning for examination until I release you to full duty."

The surgeon wrote out the order and handed it to Charlie. "Give this to your lieutenant."

***

Charlie entered the tent area of his platoon to see most of his fellow troopers gathering around Sergeant O'Brien, a fair enough fellow for a sergeant. As he drew close to the group, he heard Billy Branham speak to O'Brien. "Sergeant, we've been talking about why we're down here fighting the Mexs. Some say to keep them from taking Texas back. But Cooper there", Billy chucks a thumb at the man, "said he heard Lieutenant Penn say were fighting for something called Spoils of War. What does that mean?"

Obrien spoke. "That's the reason we're here sure enough, Spoils of War."

The men leaned toward the sergeant and waited expectantly.

"Spoils of War has been around forever. It means whoever wins a fight can take whatever he wants from the looser. His gold, his land, his women."

"Wow, that sounds good to me," Billy said. "I saw several silver things in some of those houses we broke into during the fighting in town."

"I sure saw some pretty girls I'd like to get hold of," another trooper said.

O'Brien spoke quickly. "I don't mean you can steal things from the Mexs. And sure as hell don't get caught doing it for It'd go damn hard for you."

"Then what do I get for fighting?" Billy said.

"Eight dollars a month," O'Brien said.

"And a good chance to get killed," a trooper said in a hard voice.

A hard chuckle ran through the group of men.

O'Brien gave the men a sweep of his eyes. "This fighting is all about land. About taking land from the Mexs like the Texans did."

"How much land?" Charlie said.

"I have no idea," O'Brien said. "Could be all of Mexico. General Taylor will decide that. Or maybe President Polk back in Washington."

"So we're fighting and dying for Mex land," Charlie said.

"That's the size of it," O'Brien said.

"Doesn't sound right to me," Charlie said.

"Who said it was right." O'Brien gave Charlie a look. "That's just the way it is."

"There has to be some way I can get my share," Billy said thoughtfully.

"I didn't hear that," Obrien said. "And get this straight, don't get caught taking things or you'll be a sorry bastard."

***

Charlie stared down at the city of Monterrey with its great walls that had been so difficult and costly for the Americans to breach. He had climbed the hill from which he had first viewed the city days earlier. At first glance,

47

the walls appeared untouched. Upon closer inspection, he saw narrow gaps in the walls, their stones lying in broken piles on the ground. Those openings would be the work of the American's 18-pounders and places where the Americans had finally broken into the city. He turned his sight to Fort Diablo where he had fought. He could see no damage to the structure, yet it had been taken.

He turned and made his way down from the top of the hill. Near the bottom he came upon a grove of young trees. A sapling one and one half inch in diameter at its base caught his attention. It had a wide u-shaped branching about six feet up its length. He dug a knife from his pocket and cut the sapling off close to the ground. He had a use for such a piece of wood.

***

Charlie entered the hospital tent of the Mexican prisoners. He was carrying the crutch that he had made from the sapling found the day before. He had peeled the bark off the wood, shaped and smoothed the u-shaped crotch and guessed at the proper length. He continued on between the rows of beds with their wounded occupants to the one of the soldier who had fought him. The man lay staring at the ceiling. He paid no attention to Charlie, as if he had not appeared, did not exist.

Charlie spoke not a word. He silently leaned the crutch against the bed near the man's hand and turned and walked away between the rows of cots. He had proceeded but a short distance when the Mexican called out.

"Wait."

Charlie halted and turned to look. The man was sitting on his bed and holding up the crutch.

"Why this?"

"Thought you might need it one day."

The man placed the crutch under an arm and rose to standing position.

"I can use it now."

"That's good."

Several seconds passed as they stared across the distance at one another.

"What do you want in return?"

Charlie spoke in a calm voice. "Just to talk. But not about fighting."

"Just talk," said the man.

Charlie returned the few steps to the Mexican.

"My name's Charlie Bell." Charlie held out his hand.

The man raised a hand and shook Charlie's.

"Mine is Ernesto Armentes."

Charlie was surprised at the size of the man standing nearly a head shorter and slender. The courage and strength of his bayonet fighting had made him seem a larger man.

"How is it that you speak my language?"

"A blacksmith in Corpus Christi taught me. How's the leg?"

"It'll heal but I'll have a limp."

Silence held.

Ernesto spoke. "What will they do with me?"

"If you're lucky, you'll be traded for some American who was taken prisoner by your people. "

"And if not?"

"You'll be held with the other prisoners."

"How long?"

"Until the war is over, I'd guess."

"That could be years for my people will not surrender."

The sound of a bugle, the notes clear and sharp, swept across the camp.

"There's the call to chow," said Charlie. 'I'd better be going for they don't hold it for anybody."

Charlie hesitated. "I'll drop by again and see how you're doing."

Ernest said nothing.

Charlie turned and left the tent.

***

"When I'm released after the war I'll go home to Santa Fe," Ernesto said in reply to a question from Charlie. "Where will you go?"

"I don't know. Maybe back to Corpus Christi."

In the morning of the fifth day after the battle for Monterrey, Charlie had gone with a pleasant feeling to the hospital of the Mexican prisoners. Ernesto had made a small smile and lifted a hand in greeting. Charlie had been surprised by that smile. Then the understanding came, he too would be glad to see a friendly face among Mexicans captors should he be one of their prisoners.

"Tell me about Santa Fe."

"It's a beautiful town in the Sangre de Christos. I have a father and a young sister there on our little rancho by the Rio Grande. We raise sheep and vegetables that we sell in the town."

"Sounds like a nice place," Charlie said.

Ernesto spoke in a hopeful tone. "I know a little English for there are Americans there and I've sold vegetables to them. I would like to learn more. Maybe you would teach me."

"Be glad to." Charlie was pleased that Ernesto was well enough to want to learn English. "But not today, I'll come by tomorrow and we can start. And you can teach me some more of your language too." Charlie was glad that Ernesto had accepted him as a friend. He turned and left the hospital with a light step. The painful throbbing in his head had lessened. Was that due to the friendliness of the Mexican soldier?

The last week of September passed with Charlie growing ever stronger. His headaches were occurring less frequently and with lessening intensity. He spent his afternoons visiting with Ernesto in the hospital tent of the Mexican prisoners. Using Charlie's knowledge of Spanish as a base, they had begun teaching each other their language. Charlie's ear was becoming ever more attuned to the spoken Spanish and his tongue to speaking it with less of an accent.

Charlie discovered Ernesto was a likeable fellow, quick to laugh at Charlie's efforts to speak a new word, and at his own attempts to speak English. Ernesto's friendliness quickly erased Charlie's feeling of strangeness from becoming a friend of a man he had tried to kill. Ernesto told that he was nineteen years old and had left Santa Fe shortly after General Kearney and his Americans had captured the town on August 8 this year. He had joined the Mexican Army with five other men and journeyed with them to Monterrey.

Chapter Four

Charlie entered the mess tent, received his food and looked about for a table. He saw half a score of sergeants, with Sergeant O'Brien among them, at the table reserved for the sergeants of the 57th. Usually the sergeants were telling jokes and laughing and kidding each other, but now every face held a glum expression.

Charlie crossed to the table nearest to the sergeants and sat down with his food. As he ate, he listened closely to what was being said that would cause them to have such sour expressions.

"That can't be true, Tolliver," Obrien said.

'That's what Cadwall told me he heard," Tolliver replied. "Said he heard it when he went to report to Lieutenant Hopkins. The 57th has been ordered to join General Scott for his attack on Mexico in the south."

"When," said O'Brien.

"We leave in five days," said Tolliver.

"How the hell are we going to get there?" said another sergeant.

"We're to march to the Gulf and go aboard ships that'll be waiting," Tolliver said.

"Our men won't like this," O'Brien said.

"Hell, I don't like it," said a fourth sergeant.

A young sergeant spoke with a half joking tone. "I've always wanted to take a ocean voyage. This 'pears to be my chance."

The other sergeants gave the man a sour look.

Charlie sat chilled by what he had heard. He had believed he was finished with fighting after the capture of Monterrey. How wrong he had been. He stuffed the two biscuits of his meal into a pocket and ate the remainder of the food to the last crumb.

***

Charlie entered the officer's area of the encampment. A lieutenant gave him a questioning look as to why he was there. Charlie saluted and asked the location of the tent of Captain McIntosh of the 5th Infantry. The officer pointed out the tent. Charlie continued on.

The tent stood open and Captain McIntosh was visible seated at a small table and writing. Charlie knocked on the canvas.

"Captain McIntosh, sir," Charlie called.

The captain looked up from his writing and at Charlie. "What is it trooper?"

Charlie noted there was no sign of recognition, no remembrance of having ordered Charlie to kill a man, the

Lancer Captain, and that Charlie had lifted his musket and did as ordered.

"Lieutenant Randall said I should see you, sir?"

"Come in."

Charlie ducked his head and entered the tent and saluted.

"What's you name trooper?"

"Charles Bell, sir. Lieutenant Randall said I should talk to you."

"What about?"

"Getting released from the army, sir"

"Is your enlistment ended?"

"No, sir. Over a year left. But I still want out."

McIntosh frowned. "Many soldiers feel that way. But I can't release you for that reason."

"I know that. But I'm just sixteen years old and that should get me out."

"That'd do it, if it's true." The captain focused on Charlie's face, examining it closely, the thin blond fuzz of a beard, the tallness of him. "Can you prove your age?"

"No, sir. But that's my real age."

"Then you lied to the enlistment officer?"

"Yes, sir."

"But you're telling the truth now?"

"Yes, sir."

"I'd say that you've heard about the 5th Infantry being transferred to General Scott's army?"

Yes, sir."

"And now you don't want to fight again?"

"I wanted out before that." Charlie didn't like the way this was going.

"Request denied, Private Bell. You must serve out your entire enlistment."

"But, sir…"

"That's enough, Bell. You're dismissed."

Charlie remained in place, preparing to argue the denial.

"You're dismissed, Bell," McIntosh said, his voice flinty.

Charlie saluted, pivoted and left. As he moved away, he made a wry smile. Captain, you are wrong. I will not serve out my enlistment.

***

Charlie walked back through the encampment toward his tent area. With the thought of another war with months of fighting heavy on his mind, he barely noticed the other troopers moving about. He wanted no more fighting. He must leave the army and get out of Mexico. He halted and looked to the north. Corpus Christi lay there some five hundred miles distant, with every mile through Mexican land where every man would want to shoot him. His size, fair skin and blond hair would make him an easy target.

A plan came to Charlie. After every battle, General Taylor ordered all the weapons taken from prisoners or left behind by the retreating Mexicans, be gathered up so that they would not fall into the hands of men who would use them against the Americans. Charlie knew the location of a tent holding those pistols, swords and other military items by the scores. He changed course and a short walk later, he came to the tent.

He recognized the armed guard stationed at the entrance of the tent and called out. "Baker, have you heard the latest news?"

"What news?"

"The 5th Infantry is to be sent to join General Scott to fight in the south." Charlie continues to draw closer.

"You're joshing me."

"God's truth."

"Damnation. I don't like that."

"Me either. But that's it."

"When do we leave?"

"Just five days. We march to the coast where ships will carry us down there."

"Well, five days is five days. I've got a problem that needs attention right now. Would you stand my post for a few minutes while I go to the latrine?"

"Sure. I got a few minutes."

"Thanks. Won't be long."

Baker handed his musket to Charlie and hurried away.

Charlie quickly entered the large, shadow filled tent and found it heavy with a strong odor of iron, gun smoke, dirty cloth, damp leather. Scores of muskets, pistols, cartridge boxes and backpacks and blankets lay before him in large disordered mounds, having been cast down without care from the wagons that had hauled them from the battlefield. He felt dismayed at the lack of care for the firearms. They should have been cleaned and oiled to prevent rust.

Spoils of War, thought Charlie as he viewed the Mexican plunder. He made a brief hard smile at the thought. He would take his share now.

He hurriedly moved to the pile of muskets, pistols and cartridge boxes. Many of the muskets had bayonets attached; one was stained with what he judged to be blood. The sabers were long gone, for they were prize possessions, with American officers always quickly taking them as trophies.

He sorted through the weapons, ignoring the muskets for they were too big and visible for what he planned, and instead chose, after close inspection, a single shot cap and ball pistol and a holster and belt for it.

He paused as a thought came to him. He had but eight dollars from his last pay and a few pieces of silver remaining from the previous one. He needed more than that to buy food for the coming journey. Nothing could be more easily sold during war than a weapon. He chose a second pistol and holster. He turned next to the cartridge boxes, and searching through the contents of several, filled one with charges of powder, lead balls, and firing caps for the pistols.

Satisfied with the items, he carried the items to the rear of the tent and placed them on the ground close against the canvas wall. Just above them, he cut a slash in the canvas some half foot long and large enough for him to find in darkness.

He hurried back to his post at the entrance of the tent and took up Baker's musket and waited for the man to return.

***

Charlie lay silently on his cot in the darkness of the tent and waited for the night to grow old and the five troopers sharing it with him to sleep. In the close con-finement of the tent, all sound seemed magnified, the creak of cots as men stirred, the rustle of their blankets, the low sigh of their breathing, and now and again a muttered word or two from dreamers.

Finally satisfied that all were asleep, Charlie arose and drew on his uniform. He pulled his partially full pack from under his cot. Every day since leaving the hospital, he had stored a portion of his rations in the pack in preparation for this journey. He added a full canteen of water, rolled up his blanket, tied it tightly and fastened it to the top of the pack.

He shouldered the pack and stole silently along the narrow passageway between the rows of cots and stepped outside. He halted and studied the camp with its scores of tents all dark and silent. He saw no sign of the roving sentries that patrolled the camp at night.

Overhead the sky held large black clouds drifting south upon the back of an invisible wind. He was glad for the clouds. A half-moon was finding small openings between the moving clouds and playing "see me now and see me not" and briefly illuminating the camp with its silver-gold rays of light. Tonight, Charlie didn't like the moon.

He moved away toward the tent where his pistols and ammunition were hidden. His heart sped its beating, for to be caught deserting in time of war would bring execution before a firing squad.

As he moved on, a pair of sentries of the roving patrol came into sight and moving toward him. He hurriedly hid in the shadow of the closest tent. When they had passed by and out of sight, he moved warily on.

Charlie came within view of the tent holding his stash of captured Mexican weapons. Waiting until the guard stationed there was facing away, he stole ahead to the tent and continued along its side and sliding his hand on the canvas, searching for the cut he had made. His fingers found the marker and he dug out his knife and quietly enlarged the cut and inserted his hand. Had his stash of weapons been found? Would his hand be grabbed and he made a prisoner?

His fingers touched the pistols and he breathed a sigh of relief. He pulled the weapons in their holsters and the cartridge box with its shoulder strap to the outside, swiftly loaded all into his pack and shouldered it. Moving from the shadow of one tent to the shadow of another, he made his way toward the north border of the encampment. In a grove of trees, he halted in their deep shadow. Now he must get past the sentries patrolling the outer perimeter without being seen.

He turned and looked north where hundreds of miles distant lay Corpus Christi and Ayers and his blacksmith shop and his cot in the rear where he had slept so many nights. Then farther north more hundreds miles lay Santa Fe that Ernesto had talked about.

He cast a last look back at the camp and found it lying dark and silent with the moon continuing to play its game of "see me now, see me not" with the earth. In a brief moment of moonlight, his eye caught movement among the tents, a man walking with a hobbling, bobbing step. Charlie saw the man's course would bring him close and he stood unmoving in the deep darkness among the trees and waited.

A few short minutes passed, and with the man close, Charlie called out in a low voice. "Ernesto, where're you going?"

Ernesto jerked to a stop and whirled to look in the direction of the call.

"That you, Charlie?"

"Sure enough is."

"Madre de Dios, you gave me a scare."

"Now where in hell are you going so late at night?"

"Just taking a little walk."

"Maybe all the way to Santa Fe?"

"Maybe that far."

"How did you get away from the hospital?"

"The guards were talking and I just walked away. What are you doing here? Are you on sentry duty?"

"No. Just out for a walk same as you."

"To Corpus Christi?"

"No. Just north."

"Will they search for us," Ernesto asked worriedly.

"Not you. But they'll come looking for me so that they can put me before a firing squad."

Ernesto stared silently at Charlie.

"Let's see if we can get past the sentries," Charlie said.

Charlie led the way to the edge of the grove of trees where they hid and silently watched for movement in the darkness. Shortly, two sentries carrying muskets emerged out of the gloom on their left, crossed in front of them a few feet distant and onward to vanish back into the night on the right.

"Let's put some distance behind us," Charlie said.

He led the way from the woods and into a grassy plain and onward with a gentle north wind washing away the stench of the encampment with its thousands of men jammed close together, the rank stink of scores of open latrines, the droppings of hundreds of horses fenced close by, and replacing all with the clean fresh odor of growing grass and the scent of unsullied earth.

Charlie drew in a deep full breath of the air, and held it for a time before expelling it. So delicious was the air that he drew in a second and held it for a longer time, savoring it as he would fine food, before he allowed it to escape back into the darkness of the night. Those breaths gave him a most pleasant feeling of being free.

Ernesto followed Charlie, leaning on his crutch and favoring his injured leg. He tried to keep up with his comrade's long strides and failed.

Charlie looked back at Ernesto, and seeing he was falling behind, slowed his pace.

They moved on with the moon now and then giving them a view of the land that lay ahead.

Minutes later Charlie and Ernesto came upon El Camino Real, "The King's Highway" the road that connected Monterrey to the land that lay to the south to Mexico City, and to the north all the great distance to Alta California.

Ernesto leaned on his crutch and rested. "Best that you go on alone," he said. "I'm slowing you too much."

"It's alright. We can watch for any troopers that might be coming and stay out of sight."

"Don't worry about me. The people will hide me if I need it."

Ernesto was correct about himself being safe. However, Charlie was surrounded by Mexicans who would shoot him. Further, should American troopers capture him; he would be in serious trouble. Charlie was the one in big need of help.

Ernesto studied Charlie in the frail light of the moon. "Let's travel together. I'll tell my people that you helped me escape from the Americans. Then they won't shoot you."

"That just might work."

"Why not come to Santa Fe with me?"

Charlie considered the offer. It would be very unlikely for the army to search for him in that faraway place.

"I'll come. I want to see this town you've brag about."

"It's a long distance."

"We have all the time in the world. "

"No we don't. Let's travel" Ernesto said quickly.

They walked away upon the ancient road, El Camino Real, rutted and eroded by decades of use by feet, hooves, and iron rimmed wheels.

***

When the first rays of the sun fell upon Charlie and Ernesto they turned aside and found a secluded place on the side of a low hill out of sight of anyone passing by on the road.

Ernesto immediately sat down on the ground, stretched out his legs and made a deep sigh. "Hard work walking with a crutch," he said in a tone that hinted at an apology to Charlie.

"I'd sure think so."

Charlie hadn't had a headache in the past three days and felt strong. He wanted to continue on and be far away from the American Army as quickly as possible. Still, as he studied Ernesto's strained and sweaty face, he felt no resentment toward him for he was a game fellow.

"How long for us to get to Santa Fe?" Charlie said, dropping his pack onto the ground.

"It took us five weeks getting here and that was riding on a wagon. With me walking on a crutch, it'll take twice that long going back."

"Tell me about the country."

"We'll go west across the Sierra Madre Oriental. That's those tall brown mountains you see way off there miles ahead."

Charlie looked at the mountains with their dark, jagged peaks etched against the blue sky and stretching north and south as far as he could see. The road they traveled wound through green colored hills that grew ever taller until they merged with the flanks of the mountains. Many long days of walking would be needed to reach their tops.

"There'll be bandits up there who'll try to rob us."

Charlie gave Ernesto a grin. "What do we care about a few bandits when we once had a whole army trying to kill us?"

Ernesto matched Charlie's grin. "We'll still need guns."

"I can fix that."

Charlie dug the holstered pistols from his pack.

"How did you get them?" Ernesto asked.

"I earned them fair and square."

He removed the cartridge box from his pack and opened the lid and began loading one of the pistols, pouring gunpowder down the barrel, shoving wadding and lead ball down tightly on top of the gunpowder with the short ramrod, removed from under the barrel, and pressed the primer cap over the nipple.

He handed the pistol to Ernesto. "Yours.

Charlie turned to loading the second pistol. He enjoyed the weight and the feel of the weapon in his hand. Finishing the task, he shoved the pistol into its holster.

"Tell me about the rest of our trip," Charlie prompted Ernesto.

"Once we're over the mountains we'll come to Saltillo. Then comes Torreon. Altogether, that's about two hundred miles. Then we'll pass through a town called Chihuahua, then Ciudad Juarez on the south side of the Rio Grande and El Paso on the north side. EL Camino

Real forks there at El Paso. One fork turns west to California; the other goes straight north to Santa Fe. Altogether, the distance for us is about twelve hundred miles."

"We sure need horses," Charlie said.

"They cost money and I have only a little silver. How much do you have?"

"Eight dollars and some change. And I have a little food. Let's have a bite."

Charlie dug into his pack and brought out a half ration, consisting of a biscuit and a hand-size piece of dried beef. These he broke into equal shares and handed Ernesto his.

"We'll make what I have last us as long as we can."

Ernesto checked the size of his portion. He broke off a section from both the biscuit and the meat and held them out to Charlie. "We divide it according to size."

Charlie shook his head. "Maybe later. When you're stronger." Charlie felt protective of the smallish fellow that he had tried to kill and would have killed had their fight lasted a moment longer. Perhaps it was also because they had shared an exploding cannon ball and both been wounded. Now he would do his best to see that he reached home safely.

"This looks like a good place to take a nap," Charlie said.

He spread the blanket upon the ground and lay down on half of it.

Ernesto lay down on the second half.

Charlie looked up at the sky. The clouds of the night had ridden the wind off to some unknown place in the south and the sun now held dominance of the heavens.

He closed his eyes to rest. Memory of past events came flooding to the forefront; working with Ayers at the hot forges, the journey with the general on his white horse from Corpus Christi to Matamoros, then to Monterrey, and all the battles he had fought along the way. The battles and the killings that had only one purpose, to take another people's land.

Charlie caught the flood of memories and halted them. A new life lay ahead with never before seen mountains and valleys, towns and their people, unknown and guessable adventures with a new friend. With those thoughts, Charlie rested while Ernesto slept.

***

Charlie jerked awake and hastily looked about. They were alone and he relaxed somewhat. Still, he had fallen asleep and that was dangerous. He checked the sun and found it half way to its zenith. Valuable travel time had been wasted.

"Ernesto, time to go."

Ernesto immediately came awake and sat up. "Everything all right?"

"Time we get moving."

Ernesto, using his crutch, rose to his feet. "I'm ready."

Charlie speedily rolled his blanket and fastened it to his pack. He shouldered the pack, and hung the cartridge box over his shoulder where it would be ready to his hand should he need it for a quick reload of their weapons.

Charlie, shortening his stride to that of Ernesto's limping step, led the way to the road. They turned west toward the mountains.

***

In the early afternoon, Charlie heard the sound of a horse's hooves and the crunch of iron wheels of a vehicle on the stony roadway and overtaking Ernesto and himself. He cast a look behind and saw a buggy, pulled by a quick-stepping trotting horse of a dark gray color, closing upon them.

Shortly the buggy drew up beside them. The driver, the lone occupant, pulled the horse to a halt.

"Where are you two soldiers going?" asked the driver, a robust man of forty or so and richly dressed in dark clothing, topped off with a black sombrero.

"We've been wounded and out of the army and we're going to Santa Fe," Ernesto replied.

The man studied Charlie, his uniform, his face. He turned back to Ernesto. "That's a long distance," said the man. "I can give you a ride for a ways."

"Many thanks," Ernesto said.

"Thank you," Charlie said. He thought the words Ernesto's had chosen regarding their presence on the road were wise ones.

"Then store your pistols and pack in the trunk and climb in."

Charlie and Ernesto hastily moved to the rear of the buggy. They opened the trunk, made of wood and leather and strapped to the rear of the buggy and placed their pistols, pack and cartridge box inside and closed the lid. Charlie understood that the man did not want two strangers with weapons to ride with him. They climbed into the single seated buggy beside the man, Ernesto next to him and Charlie on the outside. They gave each other a look of approval at their good fortune of obtaining a ride.

The man popped his buggy whip over the horse's ears, without touching the animal. The horse broke into an easy trot.

Charlie followed the conversation in Spanish between the man and Ernesto for a time. Then he turned to watching the farms and homes of the countryside slide past. Considering the speed of the buggy, he felt safe from capture by an army patrol that could be searching for him as an army deserter. Shortly, the rhythmic clop-clop of the horse's hooves, and the comfort of the overstuffed leather seat of the buggy riding on its shock absorbing flexible iron springs, put weights upon his eyelids and he dozed. He awoke from time to time, only to drift back to sleep as the horse drew the buggy ever onward mile after mile.

***

Charlie awoke to the buggy stopping and he hurriedly looked around for any danger. They were halted in front of a sprawling single story house made of gray stone with a huge courtyard with flowers and two large trees and a flag stone walkway leading to the entrance. Surrounding everything was a waist high wall of the same gray stone that made the house.

A very pretty woman, with black hair and wearing a full-length bright yellow dress, came hurrying from the house. She waved at the man and smiled happily. The man hastily climbed down from the buggy and met her at the gate. He pulled her to him and hugged her tightly. She smiled and pressed against him.

She looked past the man to Ernesto and Charlie. Her brown eyes lingered but a few seconds on Ernesto and then moved to Charlie. She measured the tallness of him, then checked his blond hair and finally settled on his eyes. Her curiosity was a visible thing with many questions begging to be asked. She said not a word.

As time went by and the woman's eyes still holding Charlie's, he gave her a quick smile. At that, she gave him a flicker of a dimpled smile and then turned back to the man.

The man had noted the exchange between Charlie and the woman and he spoke to her. "They are quite a pair. Ernesto has told me they actually fought and tried to kill each other."

"Is this true?" asked the woman.

"It's true," Ernesto replied. "Now I have a good friend."

"And so have I," Charlie added and touched Ernesto upon the shoulder.

"Have a safe journey," said the man, telling Ernesto and Charlie that the conversation was at an end. "And should you see any bandits, kill them all."

"Thanks for the ride," Ernesto said.

Charlie and Ernesto quickly retrieved their weapons, pack and cartridge box from the trunk of the buggy.

"Saltillo is straight ahead up over the mountains," said the man, pointing.

"Thanks again," Charlie said.

"Adios," Ernesto said.

Charlie and Ernesto continued their trek upon El Camino Real to the west.

Chapter Five

"That's going to be a tough climb for a man with a bad leg," Ernesto said and pointing at the tall peaks of the mountains some fifteen miles distant.

"Yeah, and it's storming up there right now," Charlie said and noting the thick layer of black clouds that hung over the high backbone of the mountains.

"It's going to be cold too and us without coats."

They continued on mounting the ever steeper road that was lined with aged trees and farm fields fenced with stone dug from the soil so that a crop could be planted. Now and again, they passed small houses, usually built of stone with mud as mortar. Sometimes they saw children playing in a yard, their young innocent voices ringing out clearly. As they climbed higher, the land became ever more steep and rocky with patches of trees on the higher slopes. The fields became smaller and the houses further apart. Sheep were seen grazing on the hillsides. Rarely a cow or horse was seen.

In late afternoon, Charlie and Ernesto came upon a two wheeled cart pulled by a small, gaunt burro. The driver was an ancient man with a gray beard reaching to his chest. He wore worn, faded pants and shirt and a battered straw hat. A barefoot boy of six or so, equally poorly dressed, sat on the single seat of the cart beside the man. The rear of the cart held a pile of wood cut to a length that would fit into a stove or fireplace.

"Good day," the old man called out as Charlie and Ernesto moved along beside the cart.

"Good day to you too, grandfather" Ernesto said. "Would you give a wounded soldier a ride on your cart?"

The man did not reply, his eyes had fixed upon Charlie.

"He's my friend," Ernesto said, answering the unasked question. "A very good friend."

At that, the man switched his sight from Charlie to Ernesto. "My burro is very old and the load is already heavy for him."

"I don't need a ride," Charlie said.

"I'm the one who would like to ride," Ernesto said, encouraging the man to be generous.

"Then you may ride," said the man. He spoke to the boy. "Hop into the back."

"Yes, grandfather," said the boy and quickly did as directed. He seated himself on the pile of wood.

Ernesto took the boy's, seat. "Thank you," he told the man. He turned to the boy, "And thank you too."

The boy smiled back bashfully and said nothing.

The man gave Charlie a last look, slapped the reins down upon the burro's back. The animal leaned into its harness and the cart rolled onward.

Charlie fell in beside the cart and matched the burrow's slow, plodding steps.

"Where are you going?" the man asked Ernesto.

"To Santa Fe."

"That is a very long way from here. You should ride a horse."

"We surely would if we had the money to buy one," Ernesto said.

The old man smiled through his beard. "Poor people have poor ways. That is why I have only this old burro to haul me about."

Conversation ended. An hour later and two miles farther along, the man halted the cart where a narrow road branched off to the right. "This is where I leave the main road. I think you will want to go on to Saltillo."

"Yes, we do," Ernesto said.

He stepped down from the cart. "Thank you for your kindness," he said to the old man.

"No thanks needed. I wanted to do it for our soldiers." He again focused on Charlie standing close by. "Why is he your friend?"

"Because we are two of a kind," said Ernesto. "We don't want to fight and kill other men."

"Then you are in much trouble in those mountains." The man pointed a finger at the tall peaks towering into the sky ahead. "There are many very bad men in the mountains. They watch the road and take whatever they want from the travelers. But good luck to you." He clucked to the burro and drove off onto the side road.

"I'm thinking the old man is right about the bandits," Ernesto said, staring at the mountains.

"Any bandit will think twice about trying to rob two armed men in uniform," Charlie said.

"Maybe."

As they moved off along the main road, Ernesto spoke. "I have something to tell you that you should know."

"What's that?"

"I have an uncle, my father's older brother, who is a bandit."

"A bandit?"

"Yes. But he is one of the good bandits."

"I didn't know there were good and bad bandits."

"The ones that I call good bandits are the ones who rob the rich travelers, or the tax collector, or a rich ranch owner."

"And the bad bandits?"

"They are cowards and rob the poor farmers of the little they have. Worse yet, they force favors from the farmers' wives and daughters."

"Favors?"

"They make the women lie down and give them favors. You know what I mean. Sometimes the father or husband fights the bandits to protect their women. The man is killed. That is why there are so many widows."

"What about the law?"

"The constables are lazy and it is dangerous to try to catch bandits. So they do nothing."

"Tell me more about your uncle the bandit."

"I've seen him just one time when I was a boy. He came late one night to our house in Santa Fe. He had been shot and needed a place to rest and heal. I think he was hiding from some men he had robbed. He told me about bandits, their tricks to fool the person they plan to rob. How to hide after a robbery. My father became angry and told him to stop telling me those things. They argued and my father ordered him to leave. I've never seen him since that time."

Charlie and Ernesto walked on with the sun far past its zenith in the heavens and finishing its long slide downward to the tall Sierra Madre Oriental. With the day growing old, a cold wind carrying a chilling mist came hurrying down from the high realms of the mountains and struck the men and buffeted them about. They pulled their hats down tightly upon their heads and leaned into the wind and pushed onward. Their shadows lay long and thin on the road behind them.

Ernesto shivered and spoke. "It's going to be a bad night for us."

***

The sun fell behind the mountains and the gray shadows of coming night swarmed upon Charlie and Ernesto. With the darkness, the mist laden wind grew colder.

"Feels like it's going to rain," Ernesto said.

"We need to find a place where we can have a fire."

A short while later, Ernesto halted, raised his head and pulled in a long, slow breath of air.

"I smell smoke," he said.

Charlie took a deep breath. "So do I. There must be a house close ahead."

They continued on and turning a curve in the road, a very small house made of brown stone with a tiny front porch, became visible on the right hand side of the way. A path of flat stones led from the road to the house.

On the boulder studded hillside above the house, a girl clothed in a red dress, and a small gray and white dog herded a band of some thirty sheep toward a round stone corral. The girl wore a red bandana tied about her head to hold her long black hair in place. She whistled at the dog and pointed with her hand to give the animal instructions to help her herd the sheep into the corral.

"Maybe we're in luck," said Charlie. He felt pleasure at seeing the girl and dog work with the sheep. "Let's ask the people if they'll sell us some food."

"I'm sure hungry," Ernesto said.

The girl finished corralling the sheep and turned toward the house. She spotted Ernesto and Charlie drawing near. Instantly she was sprinting toward the house, the dog close at her heels. She darted into the house, with the dog following, and the door was slammed shut. Seconds later, the thick shutters of the two tiny windows of the house were pulled quickly closed with thuds.

"She acted like she was afraid of us," Charlie said.

"She probably thinks we're bandits," Ernesto said. "Let's stop anyway and try to buy some food."

They came to the stone path, guarded by a stunted tree with few limbs, and turned along it toward the small stone house. They stepped upon the porch.

"Wish us luck," Ernesto said as he knocked gently on the door.

There was total silence within the house. He knocked a second time and louder. Again there was no response. He caught sight of an eye watching him through the narrow crack between the ill fitted door and the door-jamb.

He called out. "Hello inside. We would like to buy some food. We will pay in silver. We're not bandits. We're wounded soldiers released from the army and on our way to Santa Fe."

The silence held for a moment, and then the door opened a small crack and a woman of thirty or so peered out. She warily examined Ernesto and Charlie from head to foot.

"You're really soldiers?" she asked suspiciously.

"Yes, senora," Ernesto replied. "See our uniforms?"

"Him too?" she asked and looking at Charlie.

"Yes. He's a very good friend of mine and an honest man."

The door closed and Ernesto and Charlie could hear the voice of the woman and the girl discussing the request of the men. As they waited, a strong, noisy gust of wind came out of the deepening dusk. Rain began to rattle upon the roofs of the house and the porch.

The door opened. "I believe you," said the woman. "You can have food with us for twenty five centavos for each of you. The food isn't much, just mutton stew and dried apple dumplings."

"That sounds fine," Ernesto said. "Thank you for your kindness."

"Come in please."

Ernesto leaned his crutch against the outside wall and he and Charlie entered the house and stood by the door and took off their caps in respect for the generous woman. Ernesto gave the woman a smile.

Charlie quickly added his smile, hoping that it would relieve her doubts about them. The odor of the boiling stew filled the room and his smile widened.

The woman nodded an acceptance of the gestures. The girl stood wide-eyed and watched Charlie. He thought that he might be the first blond headed man she had ever seen. The dog stood at the girl's heels, his head lifted and nostrils open and flaring as it breathed in their odors.

Charlie placed his pack on the floor, made of compacted clay of which he was familiar from Corpus Christi homes. He turned to look about the room with its few items of furnishings. There was a small table with four chairs, a single candle that weakly illuminated the room and a cupboard with two shelves holding a few dishes and pans. A pot was cooking on a little cast iron stove in the corner of the room. In the far wall, a fireplace held a wood fire that helped to illuminate the interior of the room. Two chairs and a small three-legged stool were placed before it. They would be the resting place for the family in the evening by the fire after the chores of the day had ben finished, Charlie judged. All items appeared to be hand-made. Had the missing husband been the craftsman? A door on the right led into a second room, a bedroom he thought.

Ernesto dug into a pocket and brought out several coins. He handed some of the coins to the woman. "Is twenty five centavos enough for each of us?"

The woman clasped the money tightly in her hand. "It is for what I have to offer." She gave Ernesto a smile and held his eyes with a thoughtful expression.

Charlie studied the woman as her sight lingered on Ernesto. She was quite slender and dressed in a simple blue cotton dress. She wasn't pretty, yet there was something about her that held his eye. Perhaps it was the generous, honest smile she was bestowing upon Ernesto, or the clear black eyes that showed a quick mind behind them. Most likely both added to the result, Charlie judged. Ernesto must think the same thing for he too was taking his time in evaluating the woman.

Charlie turned to the girl that was still watching him with huge black eyes full of curiosity, and also of uncertainty, perhaps even with some fear of him. She appeared to be about twelve years old, thin, but still quite pretty. She had removed the bandana, and when she moved, her long hair swayed and tumbled like a black waterfall. To his surprise, the girl was barefooted even with the stony ground of the mountain side. She was prettier than the woman; youth gave her that advantage.

"My name is Ernesto Armentes and this is my friend Charlie Bell."

"I am Rosa Sandoval and this is my daughter Elena."

Rosa hesitated a moment and then spoke. "My husband is not here. He took some of our sheep to Monterrey to sell last fall and has not returned. I think bandits have killed him. Now Elena and I must take care of the sheep and try to make a living off this poor land."

Charlie was surprised by the woman telling them so much about her personal life. Ernesto showed interest, nodding as she spoke.

"I'm sorry for your loss," Ernesto said.

"It is very hard for us," Rosa said. She gestured at the fire. "You may rest by the fire while Elena and I prepare the food."

"Thank you," Ernesto said.

Charlie and Ernesto unbuckled their gun belts and placed the holstered pistols upon Charlie's pack. They moved to the fireplace and turned their backs to the warmth of the flames. The dog came close and gave them each a second sniff. Seemingly satisfied with their smell, the dog lay down and calmly watched them.

Rosa nodded to Elena and they hastily sat two additional plates on the wooden table. A tin pitcher full of water and tin cups and the iron pot holding stew and a pan of warm bread were brought to the table. A bowl containing the dried apple dumplings was added to the fare.

Charlie thought the amount of food to be scant rations for four people, especially with two of them hungry men.

"Please be seated," Rosa invited the men and gestured where they should sit at the small table.

Charlie and Ernesto did as bid. Rosa sat opposite Ernesto, Elena opposite Charlie.

The dog rose and started toward the table. Elena caught the movement and turned and pointed her finger. The dog lay back down.

Rosa bowed her head and in a low soft voice, blessed the food and crossed herself.

She spoke, directing her eyes to Ernesto. "I hope you like the stew. The sheep was a yearling and is quite tender."

She dipped a tin ladle into the pot and gave both men a large portion of the stew and the dumplings and a much smaller servings for Elena and herself. They ate silently as the wind buffeted the walls of the house and rain drummed on the roof.

Soon as Ernesto and Charlie had finished the food upon their plates, which they did with gusto, the woman quickly gave each a second helping. When she offered them the last portion of the two foods, they politely declined. Rosa smiled at them and divided the little that remained between Elena and herself.

Charlie sat and listened as Ernesto and the woman talked, Ernesto telling about the fighting and his army's defeat by the Americans. He told about Charlie and him becoming friends and their plan to go to Santa Fe.

Charlie stopped following Ernesto's and Rosa's conversation. He looked at Elena. She had said not a word since their arrival. He had noted that upon Ernesto giving her mother money, and her mother smiling so pleasantly, she had barred the door by dropping a thick wooden plank into strong iron brackets, one bracket attached to the wall on each side of the door. Now she sat quietly on the three-legged stool by the fireplace, petted the dog and watched the flames. From time to time she added a piece of wood to the fire.

The evening wore on, the night deepened, the rain ceased and the wind slackened its strikes upon the house. A silence had fallen between Ernesto and Rosa.

Charlie thought now was the proper time to speak of something that needed to be said. "Mrs. Sandoval, may we sleep on your porch?"

"Yes, may we?" Ernesto added.

Rosa considered the request but a moment. "The porch will be wet. You may sleep on the floor by the fireplace. I will give you a blanket."

"We'll leave early in the morning," Charlie said.

"I can give you breakfast. Two eggs and fried mutton for another twenty five centavos each." Rosa's voice told of her desire for the men to accept the offer.

"We will, with thanks," Ernesto said and gave the woman a broad smile.

Rosa turned to Elena. "Off to bed with you."

As Elena rose from her stool and moved toward the bedroom, a loud knocking sounded on the door. A man called out in a rough voice, "Widow Sandoval, open the door. We're wet and cold and need a fire and food. And some other favors you can give us."

Elena began to tremble. She rushed to her mother and hugged her tightly. "It's them! It's them! Don't let them in. They hurt me awfully." She broke into violent sobs, her young shoulders jerking with their violence.

Rosa held Elena and stared with desperation at the door. "I won't let them hurt you again."

"Let us in, woman, or I'll kick the door down," the same voice as before shouted angrily. A heavy foot struck the door with a loud blow and the wooden bar jumped in its iron brackets, but held fast.

Elena's body jerked with great spasms and she shrieked with terror.

Charlie watched in astonishment as mother and daughter held each other in their fear. They seemed to have forgotten Ernesto's and his presence. The cruelty, the cowardice of the men demanding to be let in to do what they wanted with the woman and the girl washed over him in a wave of anger that seemed to burn him.

Ernesto spoke hurriedly to Charlie. "Let's drive them away."

Charlie shook his head, his eyes glittering in the candle light. "No. We'll kill them so they can't come back."

Ernesto considered that for a brief moment. He nodded.

"Get your gun," Charlie said. He moved quickly to the crack between the door and the doorjamb and peered out onto the porch. The clouds were gone and in the moonlight, he saw two men standing in front of the door.

"Two of them," he whispered to Ernesto.

He took up his pistol and extracted the short ramrod from under the barrel and tamped the lead ball down tightly upon the powder, and checked the set of the firing cap on the nipple. He saw Ernesto checking his pistol in the same manner.

Charlie whispered. "You shoot the one on the left."

Ernesto nodded and stepped to Charlie's left. He held his pistol ready.

A foot rammed the door. An angry voice shouted, just as Charlie flung the bar out of its slots and jerked the door open. He pointed his pistol at the center of the chest of a broad, square built man standing two steps away. He pressed the trigger as the gun steadied. The gun roared. Beside him at the same instant, Ernesto fired into the second man. The red flames of exploding gunpowder from the two weapons lanced out and touched the chests of the two men. The lead balls knocked the men off the porch and onto their backs in the mud of the yard.

The bodies jerked and quivered. A moan came from the man Ernesto had shot. Then all movement ceased and the two men lay quietly their bearded faces turned upward into the night.

Charlie lowered the pistol and stared down at the dead men. He felt no regrets from killing the man.

Beside him, Ernesto let out a long breath. "We murdered them," he said in a strained voice.

"No. We executed them. To keep Rosa and Elena safe."

"Still it bothers me," Ernesto said and continued to stare at the dead men.

"This your first time?"

"Second."

Rosa came up with the candle, and protecting the flame with her hand against the wind, stared down at the bandits.

"Are they truly dead?" she asked in a quivery voice.

"They'll never hurt you again." Ernesto's voice was strong.

"Good," she said and turning from the dead men to look at Ernesto. "They were bad men and they hurt my Elena."

"Let's see what they have on them," Charlie said. He stepped off the porch, caught the front of the coat of the nearest corpse and, with its feet dragging in the mud, hoisted it upon the porch and into the light of the candle. He brought the second body to lie beside the first.

"They're well dressed for bandits," Ernesto said, observing the elegantly embroidered, closely fitted clothing.

"Must be good at what they do," Charlie replied as he removed the men's pistols from holsters strapped around their waists. He laughed with pleasure at the discovery.

"Ernesto, look, these fellows had Colt revolvers," Charlie said, turning the weapons about in the light as his trained eye admired their fine workmanship. "They're ten times better than our single shot guns."

"My uncle told me that bandits should always have the very best weapons and the fastest horses," Ernesto replied as he searched through the bandit's pockets and brought out items.

He counted through a fistful of paper pesos taken from wallets and then the contents of two leather pouches.

He looked up at Charlie. "There's six hundred pesos in paper and nearly two hundred in gold coins in these pouches. They've robbed somebody and haven't had time to spend it."

The sound of a thud came out of the night as something solid struck the ground.

Charlie whirled, cocking the Colt pistols as he turned and pointing them into the darkness in the direction of the noise. Dimly, in the faint light of the moon, he saw two horses tied to the tree at the end of the path near the road.

"I'll be damned, Ernesto, do you see what I see? Maybe we can ride to Santa Fe like the old man said we should."

"I want a better look."

Charlie stuck the two revolvers under his belt and went with Ernesto along the path to the horses. Ernesto circled the animals and running his hands over their bodies, their chest, legs, judging them. Charlie examined the saddles.

"From what I can tell with the moonlight, they're both excellent animals," Ernesto said. "We can have a better look in the morning."

"And there are bedrolls tied behind the saddles and carbines in the scabbards," Charlie said. "Those will sure come in handy."

Both men began to dig into the saddlebags.

"They had plenty of powder and ball for the guns," Ernesto said.

"There's more in this one," Charlie said. "That's good for we need to practice shooting them."

"And there's a little food in this one," Ernesto said.

"A true windfall for us." Charlie chuckled.

"It's robbing the dead."

"Hell, Ernesto, look at it this way. We've been paid for helping Rosa and Elena."

"We'd better leave the horses tied to the tree until morning," Ernesto said. "They won't like being near the dead men."

They returned to Rosa on the porch with the candle. Elena had come from the house and stood holding her mother's hand.

Ernesto removed the paper money and the gold from his pockets and held it out for all to see. "Charlie, I say we give Rosa a share of this money."

"Sure, she deserves a share."

"I mean give her all of it except for enough for us to get to Santa Fe."

Charlie was surprised at Ernesto's generosity. A good horse could be bought for twenty five pesos and he wanted to give Rosa hundreds of pesos. As he looked closely at Ernesto and Rosa, he saw something was happening between the young man and the widow, and it was growing ever stronger with every passing moment as they looked at each other.

"Keep the gold for it'll spend best where we're going," Charlie said.

Ernesto turned to Rosa and handed the paper money to her.

Rosa clutched the pesos to her beast. "Oh, thank you for your kindness," she exclaimed and caught Ernesto by the hand and stared into his eyes.

After a long moment of holding Ernesto's hand, she released it and gave Charlie a sideways look.

"And thank you too," she added.

"You are a kind woman to take a chance on the two of us," Charlie said.

"Elena and I were very fortunate that you were here."

Charlie bent and unbuckled the gun belts with their holster from the two bodies. He pulled the pistols from his belt and shoved one in each holster.

"One for each of us," he said and handed a pistol to Ernesto.

As Ernesto buckled the belt around his waist, he nodded at the corpses. "Rosa must not get into trouble with the law because of this."

"Let's drag them behind the house. Tomorrow we'll find a place to hide them."

Ernesto spoke to Elena in a firm voice, "Elena, you must never tell anybody what happened here tonight. You don't want Charlie and me be hung."

"Oh, never! Never! I promise with all my heart." She looked up at the sky. "And I promise in the name of the Mother."

***

In the darkness of the little house, Charlie slept in his clothes on his blanket near the fireplace. Ernesto slept close by on the blanket Rosa had given him.

Charlie came awake to the sound of the soft pad of bare feet upon the earthen floor. In the faint light coming from the red coals of the dying fire, he saw Rosa's naked form cross the room and kneel beside Ernesto lying on his blanket. She leaned over him and whispered something that Charlie could not make out. Ernesto's arms came up and pulled her down and kissed her. The kiss lingered.

The kiss broke and Rosa lay down beside Ernesto. He rose to his knees and kissed her, with her returning his kiss. He pulled away and removed his pants. Rosa lay down on her back and positioned herself to receive Ernesto. He mounted her.

To give the couple privacy, at least a symbol of privacy, Charlie turned his back to Ernesto and Rosa lying less than a body length away on the earthen floor of the little stone house. From the sound of their vigorous love making, it appeared Ernesto's injured leg was not a handicap for him.

Charlie tried to ignore the sounds of their urgent movements and hurried breaths. He had little success. The vision of the brown skinned girls in the water of the Rio Grande came to his mind's eye. He dwelled upon the shape of their young bodies shiny from the water of the river, and their girlish laughter as they teased the Americans. A most delightful vision.

Charlie heard Rosa moan, a sound so full, so crowded with pleasure that he knew he would never forget it. Would he ever hear that sound from a girl that he might have?

The memory of Ayers and his talk about "loose women" in Corpus Christie came to Charlie. Was Rosa like those women? Why had she come to Ernesto and lay down and offered herself to him? They had known each other but a few hours. Was it due to great loneliness or because of the money taken from the bandits and given to her by Ernesto? Perhaps it was because Ernesto would be gone before daylight and what happened in the night would never be known by others. And Charlie would also be gone.

The answer came with total certainty to Charlie. Rosa was not a loose woman. She was an extremely brave woman, a woman alone and constantly threatened by bandits, a woman who must raise a daughter and earn both of their livings from a small piece of rocky mountain side. With her womanly wisdom, she understood that all normal niceties of conduct must be cast aside, that time must be compressed, days into minutes. Each moment of possible pleasure must be captured and held tightly and close and savored before it vanished forever. Rosa was not a loose woman.

Charlie smiled and almost laughed out loud for he knew that he had discovered a great truth. Life was much more complex than he had thought. Or was it more simple? In any regard, life required action to be fully lived, as Rosa had shown with her loving of Ernesto. Charlie admired her.

The sounds of Ernesto's and Rosa's love making held for a time, then ceased and silence fell and held. After a time, whispered words that Charlie could not make out were spoken between Ernesto and Rosa.

Rosa rose and moved away with a soft tread of her bare feet upon the earthen floor and into her little bedroom. The door closed.

Charlie heard Elena's voice, "Where have you been, mother?"

"Shhh, go to sleep," came Rosa's whispered answer, Quietness descended upon the house.

***

In the full darkness of the night and with sunlight still two hours away, Charlie and Ernesto sat down at the table, lighted by the single candle, to eat the eggs and mutton Rosa had prepared. Charlie noted the young man and the widow had glanced at each but once as she had prepared the breakfast. No one said a word as the meal progressed.

Elena spoke in a pouty voice. "Is something wrong? Why isn't someone talking?"

"They are leaving and there's nothing to say," Rosa replied.

Elena gave Charlie and Ernesto an intent look and said nothing.

With the meal finished, Ernesto and Charlie strapped their guns around their waists. Charlie took up his pack and he and Ernesto went out onto the porch. There they turned to Rosa and Elena standing in the doorway and framed by the frail light of the candle. Elena held her mother's hand.

Charlie spoke, "Thanks for the food and a dry place to sleep."

Ernesto spoke quickly, "Thanks for everything."

"You are both welcome. But in truth, we owe you much, much more."

Charlie and Ernesto nodded at Rosa's words and turned away.

Charlie noted that Ernesto had not used his crutch sense they had arrived at Rosa's home. Now it lay on the porch, but a symbol of his brief presence.

They immediately brought the bandits' horses to the rear of the house. There they lifted the dead men and hung them over the saddles and tied their dangling arms and feet together under the bellies of the horses. Lastly, to hold the bodies in place, they tied the belts of their pants to the saddle horns. Leading the horses, they hurried down the path to the road, muddy from the heavy rain of the night. They walked west through the damp, chilled darkness that hid the mountains waiting ahead to be climbed.

Behind them from the darkness came Elena's girlish voice, "Goodbye, Ernest. Goodbye, Charlie."

They walked silently on.

***

The steepness of the road increased steadily as Charlie and Ernesto made their way west leading the bandits' horses, with each carrying a dead body, up through the ever taller foot hills of the Sierra Madre Oriental. In the first blush of coming day in the east, they entered a heavily wooded area and began to cast about for a hiding place for the bodies.

A short distance farther along, they came upon an area of some two acres where a powerful wind had uprooted several big oak and beach trees and they lay side by side like fallen soldiers. During life, the trees had sent massive roots burrowing into the earth in all directions, and then upon being toppled, the tangled spread of roots of each tree had wrested large amounts of dirt up out of the earth and in this manner had left behind a sizeable crater in the ground.

Charlie and Ernesto led the horses with their burdens to the edge of the largest and deepest of the holes. There they untied the bodies and dumped them without cere-mony onto the ground.

Charlie sight fixed on the men's clothing. "Ernesto, that one fellow has mighty fine boots. Just the right kind for riding horses and they're about the right size to fit you. It'd be a shame to waste them."

"I've had enough robbing the dead and I'm not going to take the damn boots," Ernesto said in an aggravated tone. "You take a pair."

"I sure would if they'd fit my big feet. These army boots don't fit the stirrups good."

"Then let's get them buried."

They rolled the corpses into the excavation under the largest tree. Using sharp, strong sticks broken from the fallen trees and kicking with their boots, they covered them. Satisfied with the burial, they mounted the bandits' horses and returned to the road and onward toward Saltillo.

As Charlie rode beside his friend, he recalled the night just past, Elena's cry of fear, the killing of the bandits, and Ernesto's and Rosa's lusty love making. The night was locked in his memory for ever.

Chapter Six

Charlie and Ernesto rode steadily westward on the road that was becoming ever steeper as the foothills merged into the flanks of the Sierra Madre Oriental. Visible high above them were their towering brown pinnacles framed by a pale blue morning sky. A strong cold wind poured down from the high reaches and buffeted the men and horses. They had met no travelers in the early first daylight hours.

"It's damn cold," Charlie called out.

Ernesto said nothing, his shoulders hunched against the cold.

They had traveled another hour or so when, upon riding around a curve in the road, they came unexpectedly upon two horsemen approaching them. Both were bundled up in much worn clothing. One was much older than the other.

"Best we get ready for trouble," Charlie said.

They pulled their pistols, and holding them ready and out of sight beside their legs, they rode warily on.

Charlie saw the approaching riders also make movement that he thought told that they too pulled weapons and held them ready.

The two men, intently watching Charlie and Ernesto, continued their approach. They made brief nods as they rode past and onward.

"No trouble," Ernesto said with relief.

***

In mid-morning, Charlie and Ernesto came to a fair-size stream tumbling down the mountain side and splashing noisily upon the boulders clogging its channel. They halted to allow the horses to drink, and to fill their canteens and those taken from the dead men. They remounted and rode onward upon the road that traveled beside the stream.

Hours later, they climbed the last steep section of road and came into the pass lying between mountain peaks, each peak rearing yet another two thousand feet above them. Along both sides of the road lay large slabs of stone that had broken loose from the mountain side above and rolled down into the pass. A few steps further along a broad panorama, hundreds of miles wide and thousands of feet below them, opened up. They halted their horses and dismounted to allow the animals to catch their breath after the steep climb up the mountain side.

"Bolson de Mapimi," Ernesto said, swinging his hand to indicate the huge bolson.

Charlie cast a look down at the basin and then left and right along the front of the mountains made of broad ridges separated by deep narrow valleys, as if a great cat had reached out with its claws and raked the mountain side. He turned back to Bolson de Mapimi and drew in a deep breath of the west wind. On the east side of the mountains, the wind had carried the odor of the forest of beech and oak on the lower slopes and pine and juniper on the upper reaches. Now the wind blowing up the mountain from the bolson was dry and held the smell of dust. That did not promise an easy journey.

"This is a good place to practice with our new pistols," Charlie said. He had fired the same models as those of the bandits, when he had worked for Ayers, and felt confident of his skill. How skilled would Ernesto be?

They reached into their saddlebags and brought out supplies of powder, lead balls and caps and spread all on a large flat slabs of rock that lay close to the road.

For the next several minutes, the pass between the peaks of the mountain rang with the crash of exploding gunpowder as Charlie and Ernesto fired at targets, large circles Charlie had drawn with a stone on the sides of some of the large slabs of rocks. At first, Ernesto was awkward and inaccurate with the Cold revolver that was a larger and heavier weapon than his single shot cap and ball pistol. After a dozen rounds, his natural coordination of hand and eye came into play and he brought the strike of his balls onto the stone target with a high degree of accuracy.

"How about that, Charlie?" Ernesto said at the end of a series of shots. A proud smile lit his face.

"Damn fine shooting. Let's call this good enough for now and get on our way."

They gathered their powder and shot and packed all away.

As Charlie turned to mount his horse, he glanced at Ernesto, and found him staring to the north toward faraway Santa Fe. A worried expression clouded his face.

"What's bothering you?" Charlie asked.

"I have this feeling there's something wrong at home. I feel it in here." He touched his chest. "I should never have left my dad and sister there alone and joined the army."

Ernesto looked intently at Charlie. "Have you ever had a feeling that something was wrong but you didn't know what it was?"

"Yes, one time. When my mother died and before my father came and told me."

"Then you know how it feels."

"I know."

Ernesto swung his hand and pointed at the great expanse of land before them. "Even if we hurry, it'll take us many days to get to Santa Fe."

"Let's hope nothing happens to slow us down," Charlie said.

Ernesto pointed. "Saltillo should be somewhere down there about forty miles ahead. We can get supplies there."

They kicked their horses into motion and started the long, steep descent upon the road that wound and curved about on the mountain side as it searched for the easiest route down into the bolson.

***

The sun burned ever hotter, the wind drier, and the smell of dust stronger, as Charlie and Ernesto, rode downward alongside a fair size stream that had been birthed on the top of the high Sierra Madre behind them.

As they entered the town of Saltillo, the sun had already run off to the west and abandoned the town to shadow. They rode slowly along the street, their horses weary from the long day of climbing and descending the mountain.

"Charlie, I'm tired and my leg hurts. I say we rent a room and sleep in a bed tonight. We have gold to pay for it."

Charlie laughed ruefully. "There's another reason to stop. I'm not used to riding and my ass is damn sore."

Ernesto made a frail laugh at Charlie's words. "It'll be tough as leather by the time we reach Santa Fe."

"It'd better get tough a lot sooner than that."

As they rode along the street, several men and women turned to stare at the tall American and the smaller Mexican in their army uniforms. Now and again a man lifted a hand in greeting to Ernesto, and gave Charlie a look full of curiosity. Ernesto returned the greeting half-heartedly.

"Charlie, the country ahead is going to be hot," Ernesto said and pointed at the land stretching away mile upon mile beyond the town. "I say we trade these uniforms for regular clothes."

"I'll be damn glad to get rid of mine." Charlie had disliked his itchy wool uniform from the day he had donned it. "And we don't want people to know we were in the army and ask questions."

They halted at a clothing store farther along the street, tied their mounts in front, skirting around two small boys of seven or so playing with a string ball, entered the establishment. After Ernesto did his bargaining, they bought outfits for riding, shirts and trousers made of cotton and broad brimmed sombreros. They changed into the new garments in a back room of the store.

"Let's give the hats to the boys," Charlie said and chucked a thumb in the direction of the boys on the street.

Ernesto nodded agreement.

They gave the remaining pieces of the uniforms to the store keeper. Then back on the street, they offered their army hats to the boys playing with the string ball. Big eyed with surprise, the boys grabbed the hats, jammed them down upon their heads, and ran off laughing with their new possessions.

Charlie and Ernesto remounted their horses and rode on looking for a store where they could buy provisions for the next leg of their journey.

They had progressed but a couple of blocks when a tall, thin man with a bristly black beard and a pistol strapped to his waist, stopped on the sidewalk and intently studied their horses. After a few moments of scrutiny, he put his hand on his pistol and raised his sight and gave Charlie and Ernesto a hard, questioning look.

They had been closely watching the man as he examined their mounts. Now as their eyes caught his, they both nodded hello.

The man made no acknowledgement of their greeting. He abruptly turned and went off with quick steps along the sidewalk.

"That pistolero knows these horses," Ernesto said.

"He must be friends of the bandits we shot."

"Let's get the provisions we need and get away from here fast."

They hastened their horses along the street until they came to a general store where they bought enough provisions to bulge their saddle bags. They filled their canteens at a public well and hastened from Saltillo. They frequently looked behind for anyone following.

In a late and shadow filled hour of the day, they stopped at a farm and asked for permission from the farmer, a middle-aged, pleasant fellow, to camp in his pasture behind the house. They negotiated with the farmer and paid him a peso for the grass the horses would eat during the night. He told them to choose where they wanted to camp.

They selected a grove of trees on the side of the pasture most distant from the road. Feeling hidden from anyone looking for them, they took food from their saddlebags and sat on the ground in the dense shade of the largest tree and ate. Finishing the simple meal they spread the bandits' bedrolls upon the ground and lay watching the road.

Ernest spoke. "Charlie, do you have a girlfriend in Corpus Christi?"

"No. Do you have one in Santa Fe?"

"Did have back before the army. Don't know now."

"You haven't been gone that long."

"My father said a single week is a very long time in a young girl's life. And I've been gone months."

They fell silent and rested.

When night came hurrying from the east and filled the woods with darkness, and the farmhouse beside the road was lost to sight, Ernesto rose to his feet and spoke to Charlie. "Time to move camp."

"Why?" Charlie said with surprise.

"My bandit uncle told me that a man who has enemies, should always move his sleeping place after it was dark so that an enemy couldn't find him and kill him."

"That sounds like a damn good idea," Charlie said climbing to his feet. "It's good to know somebody who has a bandit uncle to give advice. I'd like to meet him."

"I'd like to see him again. But he could be dead by now. My dad said bandits don't live to be old men."

"Do you think he forced the women of the rich houses he robbed to give him favors? Like those men we shot at Rosa's?"

Ernesto looked quickly at Charlie. "I sure hope he didn't rob any women. And surely didn't force any to give him favors."

"I'm betting that's one thing we'll never know."

"I don't want to know," Ernesto said.

Charlie and Ernesto carried their bedding to the opposite side of the grove of trees and again spread them upon the ground. They lay down on the bedrolls and spoke no more.

Charlie slept lightly and was awake when the rising sun broke above the horizon and brought the land out of darkness. He warily scanned across the pasture and the house. Nothing moved there. He focused on the road beyond and saw it lay empty. He called out to Ernesto.

They ate a quick, cold breakfast from their saddlebags, tied their bed rolls behind their saddles, mounted their horses and continued their journey north toward Torreon.

Chapter Seven

Every day, from first light until darkness forced them to stop, Charlie and Ernesto rode toward Torreon. Charlie preferred a more leisurely pace, one easier on the horses, and on his rear. Also, he noted that Ernesto was limping heavily when on foot. Mounting and riding was hard on his still healing leg. Charlie said nothing and allowed Ernesto, impatient to get home, to set the pace.

The days grew ever hotter as they rode deeper into bolson. They stopped along the way at the widely scattered villages and ranchos and bought food. They asked the people where the next water source was ahead along the road, and then when possible, timed their day's journey to end at that place. Some days they failed to find water and would share the water from their canteens with the tired and thirsty horses that had carried them faithfully all day. In those lonely places they practiced shooting their pistols and became ever more familiar with their shape and weight, and quick and accurate in firing them.

On the sixth day of travel with the sun lying red and flaming on the western horizon, Charlie and Ernesto entered Torreon, which even in the dusk of the day, was busy with wagons, buggies, and horsemen and people on foot.

"Let's stop here for the night," Ernesto said. "I'd like to sleep in a bed for a change."

"And have a good meal."

They continued on until they came to a restaurant, quite a large one, and there tied their horses to the long hitching rail in front, already holding several horses. As they entered the establishment, the aroma of freshly baked bread and cooking meat and vegetables made their mouths water.

Charlie gave Ernesto a look. "Smells damn good."

Ernesto nodded and smiled.

They ordered a huge meal, gave the pretty black headed girl that served them a close scrutiny, ate, then simply sat relaxing and listening to the voices of the other diners in conversation. Finally they rose from the table and left the restaurant and found a livery stable for their horses and a bed for their weary bodies.

***

With the sun barely showing its yellow face above the tall Sierra Madre to the east, Charlie and Ernesto arrived early at the big general store fronting onto El Camino Real. They dismounted from their horses, tied them, and found a seat on the long wooden bench placed on the sidewalk close to the store front. Leaning comfortably against the wall of the building, they sat waiting for the grocer to arrive and open his door for waiting customers.

Even in the early hour, the street was crowded with vehicles of several sorts; drays ferrying goods about the town, a string of heavily loaded covered wagons rumbling to the north, buggies carrying business men about, workmen in coarse clothing with the tool boxes of their trade hastening to their jobs, horsemen from the countryside, and women avoiding all of them as they hastened about shopping for the needs of their homes.

Charlie was surprised at the lack of any obvious concern by the people about the war that had been fought with hundreds of men killed and the Americans ruling part of that nation's land. He did not mention this to Ernesto.

A short, chubby man appeared hurrying along the sidewalk. Seeing Charlie and Ernesto sitting on the bench, he called out to them. "Sorry about the store being closed. I overslept." He hastily unlocked the store door and led the way inside.

Charlie breathed deeply of the many odors of the store, savoring the rich aroma of several spices, cinnamon being the dominant one.

"What do you wish to buy?" asked the grocer.

Charlie and Ernesto called out the names of the provisions they wanted and the grocer hurried about gathering the items and placing them on the counter. When all had been assembled, the grocer tallied up the cost of the provisions and spoke his final tally. Ernesto counted out the gold coins and received some silver in change.

While the grocer had been busy with Charlie and Ernesto, a middle aged American and a boy about Charlie's age had entered and gathered various food items from the shelves and placed them on the opposite end of the counter.

The man now approached Charlie and spoke. "You fellows wouldn't be going north by chance?"

"Yes. To Santa Fe," Charlie replied and wondering why the man asked their direction of travel.

"I'm glad to hear that. Me and my boy are also headed north, not as far as Santa Fe, but as far as El Paso. You've probably heard that there's been a lot of trouble with bandits along the road north. I have a suggestion." The man paused.

Charlie waited silently, watching the man's eyes.

The man continued. "Maybe we could all ride along together. Four armed men would be a hell of a lot less to be jumped by bandits than two riding by themselves.

What do you say to the idea, that you and your friend and me and my boy traveling together?"

Charlie continued to evaluate the man and his son, marking their sun-bronzed faces to their worn pants, shirts, hats, boots, and the pistols they carried in much used leather holsters on their belts. Their lanky build and faces, so similar except for years of aging, showed their close relationship. They gave no signal that this was any kind of trickery planned.

"Do you know the road between here and El Paso?" Charlie asked. 'Where water can be found?"

"Sure. I've traveled El Camino Real half a dozen times. The toughest and driest part is the first five or so days riding north of Torreon. After that it gets better. And I know where bandits are most likely to hide and attack a man traveling."

Charlie turned to Ernesto, who had been listening to the conversation and had also been measuring the man and his son. "What do you think about us riding with these fellows?"

"It's a good idea."

Charlie turned to the man. "We'll ride with you. My name's Charlie Bell and this is my friend Ernesto Armentes."

"I'm Noah Reston and this is my boy Aaron."

"Why are you in Torreon?" Ernesto asked.

"We have a small ranch near El Paso. We were short of cash and decided to take on jobs as guards of a wagon train coming south to Torreon. Now we're on our way back home."

Noah turned to the grocer and asked how much was owed for his supplies.

A tally was made and Noah dug into a pocket and paid the amount in paper and coins.

Noah spoke to Charlie and Ernesto. "We're ready to travel when you are."

***

With their saddlebags and canteens full, and their bedrolls tied behind their saddles, the four men left Torreon and rode north on El Camino Real. The long miles and hot days of riding across the broad bottom of Bolson de Mapimi fell away behind them. As Noah had stated, the land was harsh, stony and dry and the towns small and far apart, often more than a day's ride between them. Now and again they spotted a few cattle and small flocks of sheep surviving on the scant grass and brush.

Noah kept his word and they found drinking water every day, though now and again that required riding into the night before making camp.

The group remained alert for bandits. At night, one man was always awake to guard the horses and to awaken the camp should danger come out of the darkness. Several times they saw a band of horsemen watching them from a distance and they readied their weapons. The horsemen made no move toward them, simply setting their mounts and allowing them to pass by.

Charlie grew to like the Restons. He felt a little envious of Noah and his close relationship with his father, their friendly conversations and in the expressions in their eyes. Where was Charlie's father, what ocean was he sailing upon? Did he ever think of Charlie?

On the fifth day north of Camargo, the men rode into a land of rolling hills. As they continued on north, they found the grass ever more plentiful, the ranchos bigger, some encompassing many thousands of acres and the herds of cattle and sheep larger, and always, alert armed vaqueros riding guard over them.

***

On the twelfth day of riding after leaving Torreon, the four men crested a low hill and came into sight of Ciudad Juarez on the south bank of the Rio Grande. They halted their mounts and stared ahead.

Aaron laughed out loud. "Almost home, dad. I believe I can smell mom's cooking."

"Hardly," Reston said with a chuckle.

"I'm sure hungry for something sweet," Charlie said.

"Same here," Ernesto said.

They put their mounts into motion and hastened on and entered the outskirts of the town, an area of small houses with many children playing, and onward into the business section of the town.

Charlie, sighting along the main street, could see the Rio Grande, and further away on its north bank, another town. That would be El Paso in Texas. Beyond the town, lay a range of steep, wooded hills, green with new spring growth.

As he viewed the two towns, he realized that he liked to see new land, new towns, new people. He was glad that he had decided to travel with Ernesto to Santa Fe.

"I'm dirty and stinking," Ernesto said. "Let's ride on to the river and have a swim and get clean first thing."

"Damn fine idea," Charlie said.

"We'll ride along with you that far," Noah said.

They put their mounts into motion and crossed through the town and halted on the bank of the river, its clear water flowing right to left and glinting in the sun.

Noah spoke to Charlie and Ernesto, "Well, fellows, this is where Aaron and me leave you. We're going to hurry on home. We've got family waiting and livestock to care for."

"And apple pie," Aaron said.

"So long, Noah," Charlie said. "I'm glad you and Aaron rode with Ernesto and me." They had proven to be good traveling companions across a rough and dangerous land.

"Adios," Ernesto said.

"So long to both of you," Noah replied.

Father and son lifted their hands in farewell and rode their horses into the Rio Grande.

Charlie watched the father and son ford the river and climb the far bank, their horses dripping water and darkening the soil. How quickly good acquaintances began and ended. He looked at Ernesto. Would Ernesto's and his friendship end as abruptly, as a simple lift of a hand in farewell? A tinge of sorrow came over him just at the thought.

Ernesto had been observing the clear, clean water of the river. "It's time to wash the dirt off."

"And our filthy clothes," Charlie said. "Let's ride up river a ways and get out of sight of town."

They rode along the edge of the river to a deep pool of water below a rifling ford. In a grove of cottonwoods close by the river, they dismounted and tied their horses.

Charlie and Ernesto hung their belted pistols over the saddle horns and then stripped down to their skin. They carried their dusty, sweaty clothing into the river, washed them, wrung out the water, and draped the garments in the sun on low limbs of a cottonwood.

Laughing in high good spirits, they waded into the river and dove into the clear water. They came up spouting water and laughing.

Charlie gave Ernesto a daring look. "I'll race you across and back," Charlie said.

"Go!" Ernesto cried out and sped off with long, swift strokes. In the water, his injured leg seeming to be no hindrance to his swift crossing of the river.

Charlie tried to overtake his comrade, but failed by several feet. They both halted lying in the edge of the river with just their heads showing.

"Where did you learn to swim like that?" Charlie asked.

"Our little rancho borders the Rio Grande. I often swam and fished in the river."

"Well, you surely beat me, even with a game leg."

"You were easy," Ernesto said with a laugh. "Now for a bath."

"Right."

The two young men scooped up the fine sand of the river bottom and scrubbed their dirty bodies. Then listening to the sound of the riffling water of the ford, they lay on the soft sand of the river bottom and let the cool, gentle fingers of the current wash over them and carry away their weariness from their long journey.

"Look," Charlie said and pointing upward at a hawk that had come sailing in from the north, and now with its head turned down and telescopic eyes searching for prey, had begun to circle in the sky above the two young men and their horses. After half a dozen circles, the bird drifted away downriver, still hunting.

"Ernesto, I think Mr. Hawk decided we were too big to eat," Charlie said.

"Acted that way."

"Talking about eating, I'm damn hungry. What do you say to riding into El Paso and getting a big steak dinner?"

"I'm past ready."

They waded to the shore, pulled on their damp clothing and boots. They swung astride their mounts and rode them out of the cottonwoods and onward into El Paso in the late hours of the day.

Charlie had heard many stories of El Paso and now surveyed it with much interest. It was smaller than he had expected based on its reputation for violence. He noted the people on the street were about evenly divided between Americans and Mexicans.

Charlie spoke to Ernesto, "If you'll order me a big steak at that cafe there ahead, I'll tend to our horses."

"That's a fair trade."

"Get me a big piece of something sweet for desert."

"Right,"

They stopped in front of the restaurant. Ernesto swung down to the ground and handed the reins of his horse to Charlie.

"See you in a little bit," Charlie said and put his horse in motion along the street and looking for a livery stable.

***

Ernesto entered the restaurant and found it deeper and wider than it appeared from the outside. It was full of diners, all gringos except for one large table where five tough looking Mexican vaqueros, all wearing pistols, sat and silently ate. The rumble of the men's voices filled the big room. The aroma of cooking food made Ernesto's mouth water.

He looked about for an empty table, and spotted a small one with two chairs in the rear near the kitchen. He was lucky for it was the last one. He made his way to the table and sat down. It was good to rest his injured leg. Charlie must never know just how much the leg ached when riding.

F.M. Parker

A middle age Mexican woman wearing a long yellow apron came to his table. "What may I get for you, senor," she asked in a pleasant voice.

"Two large steak dinners, one for me and one for my partner." Ernesto pointed at the empty chair across from him. "He will be here in a few minutes. What kind of sweets do you have?"

"Chocolate cake and vanilla custard pie," replied the woman.

"Make it chocolate cake for both of us, and make it big pieces, and bring us coffee."

The woman nodded and hastened away toward the kitchen.

With the prospect of a good meal soon to come, Ernesto settled back and looked about at the other customers in the restaurant. From time to time he caught a few words of their conversation.

He noted two large Americans, with full beards and wearing riders' clothing with broad brimmed hats, enter and stand scanning the people at their tables. A disappointed look came over their rough faces.

The larger man's eyes fell upon Ernesto and he spoke to the second man, who nodded. They wound a path through the tables, their boots thumping the wooden floor, their spurs jangling. They stopped at Ernesto's table and stared down at him.

"Wiley, I think this table will do just fine," said the larger man.

"I sure do, Clagget. Just as soon as the fellow gets his Mexican ass up off that chair so we can sit down."

For a moment, Ernesto was stunned by the man's words. Then his anger at the man's insult loosened his tongue. "This table is mine and my partners."

"I don't see any damn partner," Clagget said

"He'll be here any minute now. And so will our steaks."

"It wouldn't mean anything to us if he was here," Wiley said with a grin.

"Get on your way," Clagget said and motioned with his thumb toward the entrance. "We're damn hungry. And we'll do you a favor, we'll eat your steaks. Right, Wiley?"

"You're right as rain."

"Find you own table," Ernesto said angrily.

"As any fool can see there ain't no empty table," Clagget said.

"Maybe all you need is us to help you to the door," Wiley said, his voice a chuckling threat.

"I'm keeping this table."

With his heart thudding in his chest, Ernesto rose to his feet and faced the men. He put his hand on his pistol.

Charlie had entered the restaurant and had seen the two men talking with Ernesto. He knew Ernesto's expressions, and when he rose to his feet and put his hand on his gun, Charlie knew there was trouble. He felt a chill as he hastened across the room with swift strides and came up behind the two men.

"My partner is right behind you," Ernesto said and looking past the two men at Charlie. He felt the pounding of his heart take a slower beat. Charlie's size and his willingness to fight made the odds even.

"What's the problem?" Charlie asked in a curt voice.

"These men are trying to take our table. Said that they'd eat our steaks too."

Charlie stepped past the men and pivoted to stand beside Ernesto. He put his hand on his pistol.

"We're keeping the table."

"Anybody who'd partner with a Mex, don't deserve a table when white men need one," Wiley said. "Go find yourselves a Mex place to eat."

Charlie felt the heat of anger wash over him. He spoke, his words brittle. "Ernesto is worth more than both of you. Now get the hell away from us."

Clagget looked from Charlie's pistol to Ernesto's. He raised his sight and looked into Charlie's eyes. "Have either one of young buckos ever shot a man?"

"Not since those two bastards we shot a few days ago down in Mexico," Charlie replied and stared directly into Clagget's eyes.

"Clagget they're bluffing," Wiley said. "Let's just grab them by the seat of their pants and hustle them outside."

"Wiley is right, you're all bluff," Clagget said.

"Ernesto, just like at Rosa's," Charlie said.

"Just like at Rosa's," Ernesto said and prepared to draw his pistol and shoot.

"Do as the young fellows said," a man's harsh voice sounded from behind Clagget and Wiley. "I don't want any shooting and bullets flying around while I'm eating."

"And who in hell ask you to butt into this," Clagget said, but did not turn from Charlie and Ernesto.

"My name's Wilson and I'm a Texas Ranger. Now back off and go eat somewhere else."

"How the hell do we know you're a Ranger?" Wiley said.

"Because I just told you! Now back off. My meal is getting cold and I don't like that."

Charlie knew the next action would come from the two men. What would they do? He tensed, ready to draw his pistol and shoot the man on the right.

"I'll just have a look at this Ranger," Wiley said. He turned.

Charlie moved half a step to the side so as to see past Clagget. The man who had spoken sat at a close by table. Charlie judged him to be about forty years of age. He was of medium size with a strong broad face adorned with a short handle-bar mustache. He wore the ordinary clothing of a horseman. His hat lay on the table opposite him. At the moment he held a fork in his hand. A half-eaten steak meal was on a plate in front of him. He seemed unconcerned about the danger his rough words might draw from the two men.

Charlie readied himself to shoot the first man who drew a pistol on the Ranger.

"If you're a Ranger, show me your badge," Wiley said.

The man lay down his fork and rose leisurely to his feet. A Colt revolver was in a worn holster on his right side. Using his left hand, he shoved aside the flap of his vest to show a Ranger's badge.

"You have a right to see my badge. Now I have the right to shoot both of you if you cause me trouble." The Ranger's voice ended hard and dangerous.

The Ranger, his attention focused on Clagget and Wiley, spoke past the men to Charlie and Ernesto who had their hands on their pistols. "You two stay out of this. These fellows don't want any trouble. They were just joking with you and your friend. Now ain't that right?"

Clagget and Wiley remained silent, studying the lawman, measuring him.

The Ranger spoke harshly. "My steak is getting cold and I sure as hell don't like that. So make up your minds, walk out of here. Or be carried out."

Clagget looked around at the men at the other tables who had stopped eating and were watching expectantly. He glared at them. He turned and spoke in a sour tone to Wiley. "Let's find another place."

The two men stomped past the Ranger and off across the restaurant and out the door.

The Ranger watched the two men until they were out the door and then turned to Charlie. "Would you have helped me shoot those two?"

"Yes, sir," Charlie replied with certainty.

"I thought as much."

The Ranger continued to study Charlie. "You said something that worries me. You talked about shooting two men down in Mexico. Did they deserve it?"

"Yes, sir."

"Why."

"They were bandits and going to rape a woman and her daughter," Charlie said.

"This Rosa, I reckon?"

"Yes, sir, her and her daughter Elena. We stood in their way."

The Ranger laughed. "Just like here, you didn't want to move."

"About the same."

The Ranger looked at the revolvers worn by Charlie and Ernesto.

"Those belonged to the bandits?"

"Yes, sir," Charlie replied.

"How about the Mexican law, they looking for you?" The Ranger's eyes were locked on Charlie.

"No, sir," Charlie said.

"That's good. Now I'm not going to ask you any more questions about Mexico. But you're in Texas now. Where're you going?"

"To Santa Fe," Charlie said.

"That's where I live," Ernesto said. "And I'll be glad to get home." He smiled with the thought.

"I'll buy your story. And I'll give you some advice. Watch yourselves when you go out on the street with those two out there."

"We will," Charlie said. "And thanks for stopping the fight."

"Just doing my job."

He looked past Charlie and Ernesto. "Your steaks are coming."

The ranger sat down and picked up his fork and knife and began to cut his steak.

The woman that had taken Ernesto's orders for the food arrived with two large platters of food sat them down on the table. "I'll bring your coffee and cake," she said and hastened away.

Charlie and Ernesto looked at each other. They did not need to speak of how near to a fight they had come, nor that they would have fought. They sat down, and like the Ranger, began to cut their steaks into pieces

After a few bites, Ernesto spoke. "Charlie, let's get an early start in the morning. I want to hurry on home and see if everybody is all right."

"I'm game to travel as fast as you want to."

"We can be in Santa Fe in four days if we push hard."

"Then hard it is."

Chapter Eight

Ernesto sat on the three-legged stool in front of the blacksmith shop in the warm spring sunlight. He idly watched the men, women and children coming and going along the main street of Socorro, the branch of El Camino Real that paralleled the Rio Grande north from El Paso to Santa Fe. A block away a dust devil was spinning up a little brown cloud on the street.

Socorro was a town of some nine hundred people, mostly farmers and ranchers. The fields and orchards of the farmers, lying to the east on the irrigated land between the town and the river, were clothed in green and studded with the bright pinks and whites of fruit blossoms. A few men were visible and working on the irrigation canals.

Ernesto had carried a stool from inside the blacksmith shop to escape the biting stink of the burning coke in the forge and the harsh clang of Charlie's and the blacksmith's hammers pounding iron. Now and again, he glanced into the shop through the opening created by the big double doors having been swung wide to allow the smoke to escape and the slanting rays of the sun to enter and add light to the interior. The blacksmith, a short, brawny Mexican was hammering on a red-hot piece of iron that he was forming into a leaf spring. When completed, the spring would be used to repair the bright yellow buggy that sat close by Ernesto. The team of black horses used to pull the buggy, and Charlie's and Ernesto's riding horses, were tied to the hitching rail close by.

Charlie was making a horseshoe. His horse had lost a shoe south of Socorro. He and Ernesto had continued on to the town to obtain a replacement. However, when they had approached the blacksmith to have a shoe made, he had told them that he could not help them this day for he had promised to have the buggy repaired by early evening. Further, he said the owner of the buggy was quick to anger and it would not be wise to fail in the task. Upon hearing the blacksmith's words, Charlie had asked permission to make the horseshoe himself. The blacksmith had been much surprised by the request; still he had agreed to allow Charlie to make the horseshoe upon payment for the iron and use of the forge and tools.

Charlie had finished with the heavy hammer, and still gripping the shoe with the tongs, was putting the final shape to the hot metal with a small hammer. As Ernesto watched, Charlie plunged the horseshoe into the tub of cooling water, where the hot metal made the water boil, hiss and explode a small cloud of steam into the air.

The blacksmith halted his hammering on the leaf spring and buried it in the glowing embers of the forge. As he waited for the metal to reheat, he spoke to Charlie. "You finished that shoe in record time, and a good looking shoe too. Would you want a job working here with me?"

Charlie shook his head. "No. Ernesto and I are going to Santa Fe."

"Too bad. I could use a helper good as you."

Charlie lifted the now cooled horseshoe from the water and stroked it a few times with a file to remove some burs left by the hammer. He took eight horseshoe nails from a box of them, a claw hammer, and carried all to his horse. There he lifted the right front leg of the horse, braced the leg over his knee, placed the shoe just so on the hoof, and nailed it to the edge of the hard rim of the hoof, carefully avoiding the tender bulk. As a last act to keep the shoe from coming loose, he bent the protruding ends of the nails with the claws of the hammer so that they would not pull free.

As Charlie re-entered the smithy to return the hammer, a Mexican of fifty or so years rode up on an excellent gray horse and dismounted near Ernesto. The man was dressed in expensive clothes; with all of it from his sombrero to his boots of a dark brown color. Silver spurs were attached to his boots. He carried a pistol in a holster on his belt. He gave Ernesto a short look and then followed Charlie into the smithy.

Ernesto thought the man, with his size and the way he moved, and his face with its full black beard cut quite short, looked familiar. He watched him as he spoke with the blacksmith. He heard the blacksmith say, "Your buggy will be ready in ten minutes, Senor Alvarez. I just have to replace the broken spring with this new one."

The horseman turned away from the blacksmith and caught Ernesto's close scrutiny of him. He approached Ernesto and stared down at him seated on the stool.

"Something bothering you, young fellow?" the man asked in a half hard voice.

At the unfriendly tone, Ernesto remembered the blacksmith's words that the man was quick to anger. Still he did not like to be spoken to in that tone. He rose to his feet so as not to have to look up at the man.

He spoke in a calm voice. "No sir, it's just that you remind me of someone I knew long ago when I was a boy. I apologize if I have offended you."

The man glanced at the blacksmith and Charlie, neither of whom were watching, then back at Ernesto. "My name is Juan Alvarez. Who is this man that l remind you of?"

"My uncle Carlos Armentes."

At the name, the man's eyes widened abruptly, then quickly became hooded, showing no expression. "Come with me," he said and nodded toward the street. "I want you to tell me of this Carlos Armentes."

"Why?"

"Just come along and I'll explain."

The man's voice was now friendly enough so that Ernesto replied, "All right."

As Ernesto limped away with the man, Charlie, who had come out of the smithy, called out from behind. "Is everything all right, Ernesto?"

"I'll be right back," Ernesto answered and continued along with Juan Alvarez.

"Why the limp?" Juan asked. "You in the fighting down south?"

"At Monterrey. A cannon ball tried to take off my leg"

"Did you kill any Americanos?"

"Yes, sir."

"That Americano back there, did he kill any of our soldiers?"

"I saw him kill one. I'm sure he had killed others before that."

"Still he is your friend? Strange."

"He is my friend."

"A good one?"

"I'd trust him with my life," Ernesto said firmly.

Ernesto halted and turned to the man. "It's time to tell me why we should talk alone."

"You will most likely tell him what I'm going to tell you. So I must ask, can your friend be trusted to never repeat what I'm about to say?"

"Charlie can be trusted. If I ask him."

"I am your uncle Carlos."

"What," Ernesto said with surprise. He studied the man closely, trying to recall as much as possible about his uncle when he last saw him those many years ago. He had noted the man's resemblance to his father. Now he decided, he could be his uncle Carlos.

"You have grown into a man since that time I came to my brother's house."

Ernesto said nothing, waiting for his uncle to tell his story.

"Here in Socorro everybody knows me as Juan Alvarez, the owner of a big rancho."

"Owner of a rancho?"

"And a bandit no longer?"

"I'm glad to hear that." Ernesto remembered the bandits Charlie and he had killed.

"Your father was right in telling me to leave his house. And further, I want you to know that I gained ownership of the rancho honestly. I won it in a game of cards two years ago in that gaming parlor just down the street." Carlos pointed at a large brown adobe building half a block distant.

Ernesto cast a quick look at the building, and then back to Carlos.

"I played an honest game. That unpredictable thing called luck was perched on my shoulder and would not leave me that whole evening. The cards just kept coming to me ever so sweetly, hand after hand.

"Then this man, who had inherited a rancho near Socorro, came to the gaming parlor and wanted to play. He was one of those soft men from Mexico City who did not work but lived off the money of relatives. When he came north to claim the land, he brought with him a new bride. He was used to an easy life in a big city with fine clothing and parties, not a dusty little town like Socorro. Further he did not like to ride and care for his rancho, worse yet, he liked to gamble. That evening when he wanted to play cards with us, he did not know that my luck was strong."

Carlos looked at the gaming place and smiled with remembrance. He turned back to Ernesto

"After hours of playing and he had lost his money, he offered to use acres of his rancho as money. I agreed with the other players to do this because the man's land was fine for the grazing of cattle and sheep. My luck stayed with me. Then this foolish man, hoping to regain all that he had lost, bet the last large piece of his rancho on a hand of cards that he thought was a sure winner. Oh, so foolish he was to bet against a man who has the luck. When I showed my cards, I had won his rancho."

"Everything was honest, uncle?"

"Yes. I give you my word as an Armentes. But then after I had won, and honestly like I said, the man called me a cheat and pulled his pistol. And of course, I shot him before he could shoot me. I had witnesses that I was defending myself and the law did nothing."

"What about his family now that you owned the rancho?"

"He had only the wife. I had heard that he beat her. I judged that might be true for at the ceremony when the man was buried, she did not cry. Once she looked at me and I did not see hate in her eyes at what I had done. So when I went to claim my rancho, I told her she could stay as my woman. You must understand she was a very beautiful woman. And since I am a handsome man," Armentes laughed and stroked his beard, "she agreed to stay with me at the rancho."

"But she could have been playing a trick on you. She could kill you in your sleep."

"I thought of that same thing. So I decided to gamble again. I gave her my pistol and told her to shoot me if she wanted to for what I had done." Carlos fell quiet and the silence held.

After several seconds, Carlos spoke again. "Ernesto, this woman is very intelligent. She tested my pistol by firing it into the ground, just to be certain that it was loaded and that I wasn't playing a trick on her. Then she said that as a condition for being my woman, I must agree that every second calf or lamb born on the land would be hers, and further that she must have her own brand to put on the animal. She said she must have those things so that when she was old and not so pretty she would have possessions of her own."

Carlos laughed and caught Ernesto by the shoulder. "Nephew, it is a great thing to have a woman who is beautiful and also intelligent."

Carlos glanced past Ernesto and quickly released his hold upon him. "Your young friend is coming to see if you are having trouble with me. Is he brave?"

"Very brave. He almost killed me before we became friends."

"You must tell me about that some day. For now tell him my name is Juan Alvarez and that I am a friend of your family. That I have a rancho near here."

Charlie, his face grim from seeing the man take hold of Ernesto's shoulder, halted beside him and pivoted to face Carlos. He readied himself for trouble.

Ernesto spoke. "Charlie, this is Juan Alvarez. He is a friend of my family and has a rancho near here. Senor Alvarez, this is Charlie Bell."

Carlos put out his hand. "Any friend of Ernesto's is a friend of mine."

Charlie shook the offered hand and held the man's eyes with his own, trying to read him. For some reason he could not define, he sensed there was something in Ernesto's and Alvarez's words that did not ring true.

"What are your plans?" Alvarez asked. He included both Charlie and Ernesto with a movement of his eyes.

"The first thing is to get to Santa Fe and see about my family," Ernesto replied. "Have you heard anything about them?"

"No. Nothing. So after going home, what then?"

"Then Charlie and I must find a way to earn a living."

"I can work as a blacksmith, but I don't like the work," Charlie said.

"I would offer you a job," Alvarez said. "But I don't yet have enough cattle and sheep to need riders. The man who owned the rancho before me had gambled away most of the livestock and I'm now working to rebuild the herds. That will take a few years."

"We'll make out," Charlie said.

Alvarez rubbed his whiskered chin and silently evaluated Ernesto and Charlie. "I have an idea for two tough young men such as you to consider." He pointed to the west toward a range of forest covered mountains some ten miles distant. "Those are the Magdalena Mountains. My rancho lies on the north slopes of the larger one."

Charlie and Ernesto turned and looked at the forested mountains standing our sharp and clear against the horizon.

Alvarez continued to speak. "Now if you go on west another twenty miles you will come to the Plains of San Augustin. It contains many tens of thousands of acres of excellent grazing land. I know that first hand for I have ridden over it. The Gallinas and Datil Mountains bordered it on the north, and the San Mateo Mountains on the south. Live streams come down from the mountains and bring plenty of water for livestock. But it is bandit country and that's why it is not owned by somebody. Men have tried to raise cattle there but the thieves always steal them. You would have to shoot some of those fellows, maybe several of them, to teach the ones still alive not to do that. You could make a fine rancho there if you did not get killed."

"We would need livestock before land was worth fighting for," Ernesto said.

"That's true. And I would give you a few head if I had them to spare." Alvarez smiled. "Of course you could steal some cattle or sheep. Young men can get started with but a few head for they have years to spend while the numbers multiply naturally. Many ranchos have been started with stolen livestock."

"We'll think about the San Augustin Plains, right Ernesto?" Charlie said.

"I like the sound of it."

"Then I will say adios to both of you for I see the blacksmith has finished replacing the broken spring on my buggy." He pointed at the vehicle where the blacksmith was hitching up the team of horses. He gave Ernesto and Charlie a smile and said, "A beautiful woman is waiting to take a ride about town in that fine vehicle."

"Adios, Senor Alvarez," Ernesto said.

"Thanks for telling us about the grazing land," Charlie said

Alvarez lifted a hand and turned away to his buggy.

"Charlie, there's still two hours or more before full darkness," Ernesto said. "We can cover eight to ten miles in that time. How about using it to travel?"

"I'm ready."

They tightened the girths of their saddles and mounted their horses and rode north on El Camino Real. Socorro faded away behind them.

Charlie looked to the west where a red sun hung low, touching the crown of the Magdalena Mountains. Beyond the mountains lay the Plains of San Augustin. He felt the land calling to him, to come and have a look.

Chapter Nine

May, Moon When the Grass Is Up - 1847

The three men rose at first light, rolled their blankets within their canvas ground coverings, saddled their horses and rode swiftly eastward upon the nine hundred miles long Santa Fe Trail, the trail that connected Santa Fe, New Mexico with Independence, Missouri. Each man had a spare mount on a lead rope. As they rode, they ate the last of their food, some jerky and raisins from their once full saddlebags.

They had left Santa Fe six days before, passed south of the Sangre de Cristo Mountains, then northeast to the Canadian River. Then east to cross the Arkansas River and Sand Creek and were now two days from Fort Dodge, Kansas. The trail, rutted and worn by years of wear from the iron wheels of many hundreds of heavily loaded cargo wagons and the hooves of the big horses that pulled them, lay visible before the men for a long distance across the green prairie-grass plain that stretched to the far, flat horizon.

On the left of the riders and a short rifle shot away, a large herd of buffalo with their young of the spring, moved like a dark brown shadow across the land with the new grass reaching half way to their stomachs. Several of the gray-white wolves, that followed the herd and preyed upon it when hungry, were within sight. The buffalo ignored the men upon their horses. The wolves trotted out of rifle range and turned to watch the riders. On the right hand at a far distance, a small herd of antelope with their eight-power binocular vision spied upon the men.

Cutter, the leader of the band of men, marked every hour as the sun made its high arcing journey across the blue sky. At his call, the men dismounted, jerked the saddle and bridle from their ridden horse, strapped them onto the backs of a fresh one, mounted and hurried onward.

The day wore away and the sun fell below the horizon and hid in its nighttime slumbering place. In the growing darkness, the riders came upon a creek running swiftly with pools and riffles from a recent rain. A large cottonwood with a wide green leaf canopy grew close beside the stream.

Cutter called a halt for the night and the men dismounted wearily and hobbled their horses to allow them to graze and yet not wander far. The thirsty horses went immediately to the stream and drank with wet sucking sounds. Thirst satisfied, they moved away from the stream and began to feed on the tall, prairie grass.

Cutter collected an arm full of fallen dead limbs of the cottonwood and built a fire, choosing the lowest spot along the steam so that the flames could not be seen beyond the creek channel. He squatted and spread his hands to the heat of the fire.

His two men brought their bedrolls close to the fire, spread them upon the ground and sat down upon them.

Speegle, a tall boney man, looked across the flames at Cutter and spoke in a half angry tone. "Cutter, I got something to say."

"Then say it," Cutter replied shortly. He didn't like the man, unpredictable, too loud-mouthed, too quick to complain. Payson had been with Cutter for five years. Speegle was new, recruited by Cutter just this spring, after a man had left to return east. He vowed to replace Speegle in Independence. Cutter had a superstition that, counting himself, three men made the correct number for his group.

"We're out of food and we're hungry," Speegle said.

"Then drink some of that creek water." Cutter motioned at the stream.

"What!" Speegle said, taken aback by the comment.

"Drink some water. That makes a good meal when there ain't any food."

"Damnit, It's not water I want," Speegle said in a harsh voice. "We've been on half rations for days and now we're completely out. I want some solid food. I say we hunt in the morning. Kill a young buffalo and cook some tender hump meat. I've got some salt to season it."

"You've had as much to eat as any of us," Cutter said, feeling his anger rising. Then in a more agreeable voice he added, "We should have met a wagon train before now and bought some food from them. We didn't. By tomorrow late we should reach Fort Dodge where we can buy supplies."

Speegle shook his head. "I've gone along with what you've said. We've rode like banshees out of hell for maybe four hundred miles and the horses are tired and my ass is sore. In all that time we've seen no humans except that one bunch of Pawnees that looked us over but gave us no trouble."

"It's not the men you **see** that's worrisome," Cutter said.

"Yeah, I know you think the army or that fellow Coldiron is chasing us because of what happened in Santa Fe. Well I don't think anybody is chasing us. The cheating saloon owner won't tell the army about us taking our money back. Even if we did take more than what he cheated us out of. And Coldiron wouldn't chase us this far even if he could track us. Hell, we only took four of his horses and he's got hundreds."

"Oh, he would and could track us," Cutter said.

"You act like you know this Coldiron fellow," Payson said.

"I know him. He comes to Santa Fe every winter and spends a couple of months while the snow is deep at his big horse ranch in the Sangre de Christo's. I've spent winters in Santa Fe too and have played poker with him at La Fonda. He's a damn fine poker player. And he's got a reputation for being one tough sonofabitch. I've seen him shoot in matches they hold in Santa Fe. He's good, damn good."

"Better than you?" Speegle asked.

Cutter gave Speegle a menacing look. "We've made him mad and that's not a good thing. Just like it's not a good thing to make me mad. Now stop your damn complainin'."

Cutter looked to the west. "Coldiron is damn good at tracking down any man who tries to steal his horses. Once he trailed his stolen horses deep into Mexico, killed the thieves and took them back."

"You think he can track us?" Lucas asked.

"Hell yes. We've done a dumb thing to make it easy for him." Cutter pointed at the horses. "We left a perfect trail for him to follow. Ever since we left the stock yards in Santa Fe, each one of us led a horse that kept the same position behind us. Two horses one walking upon another's tracks would stand out of all the other tracks.

He can not only track us but he knows there are three of us."

Cutter pointed back the direction they had come. "I know he's out there and getting close."

"Well let him come," said Speegle. "There's three of us and we sure as hell can kill one man." Speegle turned to Payson, "Ain't that right?"

Payson was looking back along their trail and said not a word.

Cutter spoke in an aggravated voice, "Do you think he'll just walk up to us and give us a chance to shoot him? He's smarter than that. He'll lay out there in the dark and pick us off when he's ready. Now that's all I'm going to say. We'll ride at first light."

Cutter rose to his feet, picked up his rifle and walked away into the darkness.

Speegle turns to Payson. "He does that every night, goes out there and sits and waits for this Coldiron. Who ain't coming."

"I feel better cause of it."

"He's starving us, damnit."

"Better not rile him anymore," Payson said. "It ain't healthy."

***

150

Cutter walked back the way he and his men had ridden until the faint glow of the fire above the stream channel had faded into the darkness. There he sat down on the thick prairie sod and laid the rifle across his lap. All day, he had sensed the presence of somebody drawing ever closer. That would be Coldiron riding a relay of his fast horses

Cutter looked up at the star studded sky where a golden half-moon drifted westward across the sooty sky and sent a frail light down upon the prairie. Its light would help him see the form of a man on horseback, or on foot coming across the flat prairie, while at the same time his seated shape on the ground would be less visible.

A bat dove out of the blackness of the spring night and darted in close to inspect Cutter. He heard the whisper of its leathery wings stroking the air close to his head as it hurried past. It made a second inspection pass, even closer, then up and away and did not return. Off on his right at a distance, Cutter guessed a quarter mile, a wolf began to yodel. It's high, clear voice rose to full strength and held there for several seconds, then fell away to silence. A wind came alive and washed over him in slow, measured waves, as if the prairie was breathing. The prairie night seemed ordinary. Somehow, Cutter knew that the night was not ordinary.

Cutter was half a century old, and regretted the events that caused him to be sitting here as a thief waiting to kill a man coming to take back his stolen property. For many years, he had lived by his wits and his gun, robbing, stealing, taking whatever men possessed that he desired. In some of those deeds, he had killed men. Most of them were honest men trying to protect their possessions. He avoided death and prison by his wits and his gun. Then he had stolen a man's wife, a pretty and desirable woman. She had lived with him for eleven days, he kept count for she gave him great pleasure. She had discovered he came by his money by thievery and had left him, returning to her husband. The man had beaten his wife severely, yet in the end he had taken her back for she was a beautiful woman. A few days later, Cutter had seen the woman and her husband driving along the main street of Houston in a fine new Phaeton buggy drawn by a pair of matched, high stepping gray horses.

He had been very fond of the woman and losing her still hurt. The memory of her lying beside him with her hand upon him and her slow even breathing after being pleasured and satisfied came to haunt him. He shoved the memory away. The day she left him was six years in the past. That same day he had vowed never to steal again. He had left Houston and traveled to Independence. There he had observed the scores of merchant wagon trains carrying cargo to Santa Fe and returning with Mexican goods. He had learned of the attacks upon them by Indians and bandits. Recognizing an opportunity to earn honest money, he gathered two brave men who were good with horses and skilled with rifle and pistol and hired himself and his crew out to protect wagon trains on their dangerous journey. The work proved to be profitable. He spent the winter months loafing and playing cards in either Santa Fe or Independence, depending upon where the last wagon train of the year ended.

He had kept his vow not to steal until six days past. The wagon train that he and his crew had been protecting on its journey from Independence arrived in Santa Fe and he had received payment, and had paid his men their share. While waiting to hire out to protect a wagon train going to Independence, the crew had set out to enjoy the entertainment the town offered in whiskey, cards, and women. Near the end of the first week, Cutter and Speegle, and three other men were in a poker game in The Emporium Saloon on San Francisco Street. The other players were Kane, the saloon owner, and two men Cutter did not know.

Both Cutter and Speegle had steadily lost. The big winner was a bald headed slender man dressed in town clothing. Cutter began to note the man often won the large pots, and rarely one of the smaller ones. Further, the man won most often when Kane dealt the cards. Cutter decided the man's luck was more than chance. Kane and the man were partners in cheating the other three players. Cutter began to watch Kane's slender white hands with the long quick fingers.

The pot of the next hand grew to several hundred dollars and Cutter knew that if he was correct in his judgment that the game was crooked, it would be now that Kane would deal a winning card to his partner. He kept a keen eye on Kane's hands. Then it happened, a small movement of one of Kane's fingers that was not needed to deal an honest hand. The man had dealt a card off the bottom. It had been but the tiniest movement, and had Cutter not been watching so intently, he would have missed it. Kane was very good.

He almost shouted out in anger to call the deal crooked, but caught himself at the last instant. He had no proof, and further should he challenge Kane by calling him a cheat, he would have to back it up with his pistol. He was angry enough to do that, but a better plan came to him.

He quit the game, having lost a large part of his pay. Speegle also cashed out and they found a table and ordered beers. As they drank the brew and feeling their losses, Cutter told Speegle what he had seen.

"Why that bastard." Speegle exclaimed, instantly angry. He started to rise from his chair, but Cutter caught him by the arm.

"Calm down. I have a plan."

Speegle settled back into his chair. "It had better be one that'll get our money back."

"And maybe some extra," Cutter said. He felt the old excitement of years past when he planned a robbery.

"What we do will affect Payson. Let's find him and see if he's game for it." He wanted to keep the crew together.

***

In the late hour of the night, Cutter and Speegle watched from across San Francisco Street as the last of the customers of The Emporium left and the drunks were hustled out onto the sidewalk and sent staggering away along the dark street.

"Let's go get our money," Cutter said. "Now hear me, Speegle, no shooting. We tie them up, gag them and leave quiet. We don't want any ruckus that will get the American Army after us." Since the Americans had captured Santa Fe months past, military patrols moved about the town to keep the peace between Americans and the Mexicans, and to protect the townsfolk.

F.M. Parker

The two men crossed the street and looked though the big front window. The gambler and his partner were seated at the poker table. They were counting gold coins and paper money piled in front of them.

"There's sure a hell of a lot of money in there," Speegle said. "Kane must've cheated a lot of men."

"That's most likely the winnings from the gambling and also the earnings from the saloon," Cutter replied. "I say we go get it all." He felt it was fair and proper to take the money from the cheats.

"Hide your face," Cutter said. "We don't want any trouble after this is over."

They pulled their bandanas up over the bottom part of their faces, tugged the brims of their hats down low, drew their pistols, shoved open the door and entered. They forced Kane and the second man into a storeroom in the rear of the saloon, tied and gagged them. Cutter had then knelt in front of Kane and shoved the iron barrel of his pistol against the man's temple.

Cutter stared into Kane's eyes for half a minute and said not a word, all the time grinding the end of the pistol barrel against the man's skull. Then he spoke, low and ugly. "Don't do something stupid that'd give me a reason to come back and shoot your ass off."

With their pockets stuffed with gold and paper money, they snuffed out the oil lamps that illuminated the

156

saloon, and left locking the door behind them with the key taken from Kane. Cutter tossed the key away into the dirt of the street.

They hurried on foot to Payson holding the horses two blocks distant from The Emporium. The three mounted and Cutter led them away, riding at a fast walk and using the night-shadowed alleyways as much as possible toward the big stockyards with its many corrals on the edge of town. To make it difficult for anyone to follow them, the men would mix the hoof prints of their mounts with the hoof prints of the hundreds of horse, cattle, and sheep tracks of the scores of animals coming and going at the stockyards.

It was then the simple plan of robbing the card cheat had gone wrong. As they came out of an alley and into the stockyards, Payson pulled his mount to a halt and jumped down.

"My horse has gone lame," Payson called out. "Somebody strike a match and let me see how bad it's hurt."

As he bent and lifted the horse's left front hoof, Speegle swung down to the ground and hurried to him. He struck a match with his thumbnail and held it out so Payson could see.

"Damnation, it's a bad gash in the bulk. Must've stepped on something sharp in that damn alley. This horse ain't going to be doing any traveling."

"We'll get you a new one," Cutter said, having noted a corral close by that held at least thirty horses.

They had caught Payson a mount, and knowing the nine hundred mile journey to Independence lay ahead of them, they had roped a second horse for each of them from those in the corral.

Towing their second horse on a lead rope, the men left the stock yard and rode south on the heavily traveled El Camino Real. A few miles later, they veered left onto the well-traveled Santa Fe Trail and raised their mounts to a trot, a pace the horses could maintain for miles.

Miles later and in the full light of the new day they halted and divided the money, eleven thousand dollars plus a little more, among them. That was when Cutter had seen the brand on the horses. It was the Steel Trap brand of Luke Coldiron. He cursed his bad luck. He changed the leisurely ride to Independence into a race to the town where they could vanish into the town's population.

Cutter pulled back from worrying about the mistake that had been made. What was done was done and could not be changed. He sat and watched the prairie as the moon slid a full hand-width across the black, velvety sky. Nothing moved upon the land except the invisible wind, and it now carried a chill that cut through his shirt and prickled his skin. Feeling weariness putting weights on his eye lids, he rose and walked quietly toward camp.

He approached whistling softly for he did not want to be shot by his men. He found them wrapped in their blankets and silent. The fire had burned down to a bed of coals partially covered with gray ash. A breath of wind had come down into the stream channel with Cutter and now fanned the coals, blowing away the ash and exposing the live coals to glow like red eyes. He knelt and spread his palms to their heat.

He cast a searching look for the hobbled horses. They were but darker shades of the night, grazing not far away along the creek. He always wanted to know where his mount was so that he could find it in the dark, should the need arise. He made his bed on the ground near the cottonwood and fell into a light and troubled sleep.

***

Cutter awoke with the morning dusk lingering and the cottonwood a huge dark shadow over him. He felt nervous and tense. He rose to his feet, buckled on his pistol and looked for the horses. The animals were scattered about not far off along the creek. Except for two of Coldiron's horses standing shoulder to shoulder but twenty yards or so away, facing Cutter.

He turned away from the horses and called out to his men. "Roll out. We've got ridin' to do."

As the men climbed out of their bedrolls, Cutter quickly tied up his bedding and turned to go and catch his horses. The two Coldiron horses had drawn much closer. Cutter thought their side by side position was strange. As that thought came, a man straightened from a stoop position behind the horses and stepped into the open. He carried a rife in his left hand and a colt revolver in his right. Cutter grabbed for his pistol.

Luke Coldiron fired his pistol and the lead bullet struck Cutter, broke through his chest bones, burst his throbbing heart and tore free through his back.

He swung his pistol and shot the man whose hand was touching his pistol. He shot the last man who was frozen in place, half risen.

Luke breathed the first breath since he had moved out from behind the horses. A chill ran through him. He had killed three men and he was alive, unhurt.

He felt no remorse for the death of the three. They were thieves and would have killed him, had luck favored them. He pulled his thoughts away from the dead men, tucked the rifle under an arm and began to reload the fired chambers of his pistol.

Luke had discovered the loss of his horses, which he had brought to Santa Fe to be sold at auction, in mid-morning when he had come to water and feed them. He had first noticed the lame horse favoring its injured hoof near the corral holding his horses. He thought it odd that someone would allow an injured horse to go without treatment. He would tend to that after he had cared for his own animals. Entering the corral, he had immediately noted that some were missing. Making a quick count, he came up four short. Looking about for tracks that would tell him what had happened, it required but a few minutes to determine several men had come to the stockyards with three horses and left with six, Four of those were his.

He had speedily gathered food and water and bedroll, and choosing two geldings, the strongest of the remaining horses, he set out in swift pursuit. He had expected to catch the thieves in two days, three at the most. In that assumption, he was badly mistaken. The thieves had ridden hard and long every day and had stayed ahead of him. Only last night as he halted to rest, had he drawn close enough to catch the smell of wood smoke of their campfire.

Now the chase was ended and he wanted only to get away from the place of killing and rest after the grueling ride.

Luke heard a moan. He cocked his pistol as he spun toward the sound.

The man moaned again and Luke stepped to him and looked down. Blood streamed from a hole in the man's chest. Luke's bullet had gone to his point of aim. He did not understand how the man still lived.

The man looked up at Luke with eyes full of pain. "You Coldiron." the man's voice was faint, fragile.

"Yes, what's yours?"

"Payson. We didn't know they were yours when we took them." He became very still as he gathered the last of his strength that was leaking away with his blood.

He spoke, his voice barely an echo of his thoughts. "Don't give that cheating gambler back his money."

"What money. What gambler?" There were several gamblers in Santa Fe.

"Emporium…" Payson's voice trailed off. His chest fell but did not rise with another breath. The expression in his eyes faded and became fixed in death.

Luke searched the horse thieves and their saddlebags and found eleven thousand dollars in paper money and a third that amount in gold. He stowed all in one of the saddlebags. Once back in Santa Fe, he would quietly investigate the man's words about the money and the gambler at the Emporium, one of the saloons in the toughest part of the town. If the man's story was correct, that they had taken back money stolen form them by the gambler at the Emporium, he would keep if for himself.

He swept his eyes over the dead men. He had no way to dig graves, and would not have dug them even if he had. Let the prairie and the animals of the prairie and the sun and rain do what they would with the bodies.

He saddled the three horses with the men's gear and put their rifles in scabbards and pistols in saddle bags. He tied the horses in a line nose to tail with a six foot distance between them. He removed the hobbles from the legs of the horses and led them to his camp not far away.

***

Luke, riding the big gelding and leading the other horses strung out behind him on lead ropes, hurried them through the morning. They drummed across the grass covered ground and splashed the pools of the streams glinting dull silver under the slanting rays of the early sunlight. Without being guided, the horses hurried along the trail they had used coming from the New Mexico Territory.

He meshed the sway of his body to the galloping stride of the gelding. The riding soothed him after the killing. He looked forward to returning to Santa Fe, a soft bed at La Fonda and a huge meal at the restaurant there.

Luke watched ahead and on all sides for Indians and white men. A lone man with ten horses would be a tempting target. He wanted no more trouble.

Chapter Ten

October, Moon When Birds Fly South, 1848

The web of darkness was weaving itself into black night when Charlie Bell drew near his destination on the mountain side. He had grown two inches in height and gained twenty pounds during the past year and a half. He was all muscle and bone from working as a blacksmith and swinging the heavy iron hammer forcing iron to do his bidding.

He slowed his long strides and stole warily on, a tall shadowy figure wearing a brimmed hat, a coat, and carrying a pack upon his back. In the night, the pack gave him the shape of a deformed man, a hunchback. He reached the chest high fence made of slabs of stone that closed the twenty foot gap between the ends of the broken rimrock. He halted and leaned against the fence and stared silently over it into the land beyond. He had arrived at this place in the early night just as he had planned. He had been here before on the same mission.

He cocked his ears and turned his head from side-to-side, reaching out for a sound that was wrong, not part of the natural noises of the mountain in the night. His eyes searched the nearby land for a form that would mean danger.

Seeing nothing worrisome there, he ranged his sight some hundred steps further away to the grove of tall pine trees standing motionless in the dead quiet air. He probed the dim openings between the trees, searching for a figure that could be an enemy.

Finally, he turned his sight to the right and to the huge gulf of Gachupin Basin yawning below him and stretching north to south for some eight miles, and half that distance east to west at its greatest width and holding thousands of acres. He could see only the basin's general outline for night had pooled black and dense in its depth and hid everything. Still in his mind's eye he saw the bottom and what was there for he had scouted its long perimeter in daylight, circling just above the rimrock that hemmed it in.

Charlie shrugged his pack off and dropped it onto the ground. From its depth, he removed a large bundle of burlap, composed of pieces pre-cut to the desired sizes and shapes. From these he chose two pieces and replaced the worn burlap that was tied over his boots with lengths of cord. The used burlap was shoved into his pack.

Using the protruding edges of the stones of the fence as toe holds, he climbed up and over and down onto the ground on the far side. He crouched there and remained motionless. He had committed himself to this thievery and that was a most dangerous decision. This was the domain of Luke Coldiron, and he protected his land and herd of horses, known for their excellence, with deadly force. To be caught by him was to be shot or hung, and then left hanging for all would-be thieves to see and take warning.

As the night grew ever blacker around him, Charlie recalled the time a year and a half before when he first arrived in Santa Fe with Ernesto. One of the first stories he had heard was the one of how Coldiron had come to own the big horse ranch. He had come into the Sangre de Cristo Mountains several years before and had happened upon Gachupin Basin while looking for a place to make his winter hunt for beaver. He had found the basin holding many horses, in fact, a number far too large for the amount of grass available for winter feed. This caused a high percentage of the horses to be stunted, and some to be crippled from fighting for food. When the spring arrived, Coldiron had ridden into Santa Fe and sold his furs. There he had purchased a large supply of powder and shot, returned to the basin and began to slay the least desirable of the horses. He killed scores that first year, reducing the herd to that number which the amount of feed could support through the winter with its snow. He had selected the ones to live that most met his standard of what a first class riding horse should be. The following year he again killed the least desirable, and again the following year. By the fifth year, he had created a herd of horses that were considered exceptional and always drew the highest prices at sale. It was told that even to this day, that in the fall he went through his herd and shot the least desirable horses. People call him 'Horse Killer', but not to his face.

Charlie stood erect and moved sure-footed toward the grove of pine trees standing silhouetted against the starry sky. As he drew close, he caught the smell of the pine needles and the sharp odor of resin. He went in among the trees and selected one on the north border of the grove. There he pulled the pack from his shoulders and dropped down to sit on the thick carpet of pine needles that had fallen and accumulated over many years.

He was glad to rest. Since morning he had ridden on horseback for twenty miles, avoiding all roads by riding cross country. He had then hobbled his horse near a spring in a secluded meadow and continued on foot for another four miles over hard and stony ground to hide his tracks.

He stared down into the black bowl of Gachupin Basin. Coldiron's ranch headquarters was down there in the darkness not three miles distant. He pictured it in his mind, the stone ranch house, quite large for an unmarried man, the stone barn where the sick and injured horses were brought for doctoring, the big round corral made of strong juniper posts set deeply into the earth, and the bunkhouse where his Ute Indian horse wranglers slept.

A cold tendril of doubt about what he planned to do came to Charlie. Even though he had chosen his path to this place with great care to hide his tracks, Coldiron was known for his keen ability to track a man or horse. His Ute Indian horse wranglers were said to be even more skilled at tracking.

Charlie made a barely perceptible shrug of his shoulders. He was not going to return empty handed. Let the future decide what would happen.

He pulled a blanket from the pack and spread it upon the pine needles. His pistol was placed on the blanket ready to his hand. He did not want to fight Coldiron, or his wranglers, but he would do so to save his life. He had killed in the fierce fighting in Mexico a year and a half past. He knew there was a great difference between that time as a soldier and now. Still, staying alive was a very precious thing and would be fought for.

He ate cheese and bread that he had brought from Santa Fe and drank from his canteen. The food was not nearly enough to satisfy his hunger; still he gave that but short thought. He lay down on half of the blanket and pulled the remaining part over him.

He had selected this spot on the border of the pines so that he could see Gachupin Basin below him and also the North Star. Now he looked to the north and found the Big Dipper and then the two stars at the bottom of its cup that pointed to the North Star. Ayers had told him that the dipper and the star made a giant celestial clock in the heavens. The North Star was the center of the clock face and the Big Dipper was the hour hand. Every twenty four hours the Big Dipper rotated around the North Star and marked off the hours of the day, more correctly the hours of the night when the stars could be seen. He would check the celestial clock when he awakened in the night to know how long it would be until daylight.

Visible below the North Star, was the outline of the topmost rocky crest of another mountain looming above him a full mile high. He knew there were dozens more mountains much taller to the north for scores of miles. They made the mountain range, the Mexicans called the Sangre de Christos, which was the southern extension of the even greater Rocky Mountains.

He lay awake listening to the sounds of the night, the swish of the pine needles above his head, the creak of wood rubbed against wood by the wind, the scurrying feet of a mouse going somewhere fast. His worry about being caught for desertion had greatly diminished. General Taylor had defeated the Mexicans in the north.

General Scott had accomplished the same in the south and had captured their Capitol, Mexico City, forcing that nation's government to sign a peace treaty surrendering much of their land to the Americans. Now thousands of American soldiers had been released from the army and returned home. He was but one of those thousands and would not be remembered.

Feeling as safe as any thief could feel, and with the bed on the pine needles coaxing him toward sleep, he cocked his ear to hear any sound that might tell that danger had come, took three slow deep breaths and went to sleep.

Chapter Eleven

In the hour before sunrise, the big male mountain lion crept without a sound through the scattering of small boulders toward the patch of bitter brush on the mountain side. The night was without a moon and the far away stars gave only the feeblest of light, still the lion with his night-seeing eyes saw the herd of nine cow elk and their calves of the past spring. The lion knew the way of the elk. They drank from the creek in the bottom of the valley during the night and then fed as they climbed leisurely up the flank of the mountain to their bedding ground in a saddle between two peaks. Their routes varied somewhat as they now and again sought a new area to feed upon, or to avoid the band of horses that also grazed the mountain side. He had but to wait for the elk to choose their course, and then he would move to an attack position and lie in wait for them. At the moment, the elk were feeding on the most tender portions of the branches of the bitter brush plant, one of their favorite foods.

The lion slowed his approach even more, one cautious step and then another, hardly moving, his tawny body but a dark shadow nearly invisible in the blackness of the night. Reaching a distance from the unsuspecting herd of elk from which he could cover in a few swift bounds, the lion halted his stalk and sank down to lie on his stomach. He was hungry and wanted to eat. Still, he was practiced at killing and now waited for that moment when the elk were not facing in his direction to make his attack. Only the twitch of the tip of his tail told of his impatience.

Again, as he had several times before, the lion turned his head and looked behind. His hackles rose angrily along the ridge of his back at the sight of the old wolf hunkered down tightly against the ground in the boulder field a few yards away. The pesky wolf had been follow-ing for the past half hour and the lion wanted to drive him away, but could not without spooking the elk. He turned back to watch the elk.

The wolf was a lobo, a loner, old and frail and mostly skin stretched over bones. For many years the wolf had needed no help to make a kill. He had been king hunter of the basin, sharing that station only with the lions of the mountain. He and the lions had avoided each other until now. Age had robbed him of his strength and now he followed this young lion and would feed off the kill after the lion had eaten his fill and left.

So old was the wolf that even the lowly coyotes ig-nored him. Except for the young males that now and again teased and harassed him, swiftly darting in and nipping at his hind quarters and then scampering away. Even with the coyotes' daring, they kept clear of the wolf's jaws that still retained enough strength to rip out a throat or crush a skull should he manage to catch one.

As the wolf lay and watched the lion, he recalled other times when he had not needed to kill to eat. That had been years in the past when he had just grown to full size. A killer human had come into the basin and shot and killed many horses. The wolf had simply followed the man day after day and ate the choice pieces of horse flesh. Many other meat eating animals, those that walked and those that flew, came to feed off the plentiful supply of food. The coyotes arrived first after the wolf, followed by the foxes. Then the noisy crows came and many others, afterwards when the meat was too old for the more discriminating taste, the buzzards flew down and cleaned up the scraps that remained.

***

The lion tensed and coiled as the cow elk came into a potion where all were facing away from him as they fed on the bitter brush. In one fluid movement, he leapt erect and hurtled toward the nearest calf.

At the lion's sudden appearance, the always alert and wary cows caught his movement from the edge of their big eyes and bolted away. The calves, trained to follow their parent, still had to react to her movement and thus were a fraction of a second behind in racing to escape. That brief span of time cost the life of the calf nearest the lion. The hurtling lion came within striking distance of the calf and gave it a powerful blow on the hip with a paw and knocked it rolling. Instantly, he pounced upon the calf and caught it by the throat with his powerful jaws. He felt the throb of the blood in the calf's jugular and the suck of breath through its windpipe. Then he clamped down and shut off the flow of blood to the brain and the pathway of the air to the lungs.

He held the thrashing calf, that weighed nearly as much as he did, and avoided its thrashing legs and the sharp hooves that could puncture a stomach and cause death. Time passed and the lion waiting patiently. When the last beat of the calf's heart came and went, he released his death hold. Leisurely he ripped away the skin from the calf's stomach and tore out the dark colored liver and ate it first, tasting the blood with its trace of salt. Then he began to eat from a hindquarter. He purred a rumble of contentment of a warm, tender meal skillfully caught.

F.M. Parker

Lying among the boulders close by, the wolf watch the lion tear flesh from the calf and eat. The wolf began to salivate in anticipation of the feast to come. His old gray muzzle grew wet and dripped with saliva.

***

The lion finished feeding and rose leisurely. He cast a baleful look at the hungry old wolf. He still felt the desire to drive the annoying wolf away. However with his belly heavy with many pounds of elk flesh, the desire to find a place to lie down and sleep was more demanding. He ambled away around the mountain side to one of his favorite places, and there to spend the rest of the night and then the morning hours resting in the warm sunlight.

Chapter Twelve

Charlie awoke with a start, his heart pounding from the abrupt awakening. He lay motionless under the blanket with all his senses reaching out to question his surroundings, to discover what had awakened him, what danger might be close. He heard the sigh of the wind and the rustling of the limbs of the pine trees around him, but nothing more. Perhaps a rotten limb had fallen and struck the ground. He relaxed, as much as possible with what he had in mind and about to do, and slowly shoved aside the blanket that covered him and looked about.

To the east, the first hint of daylight brightened the sky enough that he could see the outline of the mountains that rimmed the far side of the basin. He turned his head to look among the pine trees close about him on one side and saw nothing bothersome. Then he checked the open mountain side below him. Again nothing.

Charlie looked up the mountain side. He jerked and his muscles tensed and his heart raced as he reached out and picked up the pistol. A huge tawny colored mountain lion lay on a ledge of rock not a score of paces away and watching him. It rested on its stomach with its forepaws drawn up under its chin. There was a deadly stillness about the animal that was chilling.

What was the lion's intention? How long had it lain there on the ledge in the night from where it could be upon him with three bounds? With his heart hammering against his ribs, Charlie picked up the pistol and eared back the hammer, the metal click of the trigger spring setting sounding extraordinarily loud in the stillness. He wished for a more powerful weapon than the .36 caliber revolver to fight a lion.

With his eyes locked on the quiet, sinuous menace of the lion, Charlie shoved the blanket off and stood erect. If he was to fight, then it should be on his feet. At Charlie's movement, the lion instantly came to its feet in one fluid movement and stood staring down from the ledge at him. To Charlie the distance from the lion to him seemed to shrink by half now that the animal's full size was visible.

Time passed, and more time, as the man and the lion stood coiled for action and intently focused on each other, waiting for who would make the first move. Then the lion felt the rise of the ancient instinct of its kind that he should avoid the creatures that walked on two legs. Obeying that aged relationship, but not truly afraid, the lion gave Charlie a look from its yellowish brown eyes and leisurely stretched as if to show he was indeed not afraid and jumped down from the edge and walked up the mountainside. He gave Charlie a short last look over his shoulder, and turned back to his honorable withdrawal.

Charlie noted the full, sagging stomach of the lion and knew it had eaten in the night. He hoped that in its feeding it had not frightened away that which he had traveled so far to steal. The lion entered a patch of mountain laurel and its tawny body faded away into the night shadows still lingering there.

With a sigh of relief that the lion was no longer a threat, Charlie noted the morning was brightening rapidly and felt the urgency of time passing and lost forever. He knelt and removed a coiled thirty foot lariat from the pack and then swiftly rolled the blanket and stowed it away. He buckled on his pistol, pulled the pack onto his shoulders and directed his steps around the mountain side toward a place that he hoped would hold the object of his reason for being here. A slow morning wind carrying a chill was in his face. In the dawn sky above him, the vultures were up tracing wide swinging circles as they searched for something that had died in the black night.

***

Charlie stood in awe of the beauty of the horses in the meadow of five or so acres of mountain grass. The meadow was beautiful in its own right, framed by dark pine trees on its lower side and, on its upper reach, aspen with their white bark and leaves turned to gold from frost bite. The horses added an element of life that doubled the grandeur of the scene.

Hidden behind a large boulder, he had counted 28 mares, 21 with foals, and 7 young mares without young ones. All were of a dark color, ranging from those of deep reddish brown to those of charcoal black. He noted two mares and three colts had a splash of a few inches of white stocking just above the hoof. This band of horses was but one of several belonging to Luke Coldiron.

The foals were suckling at their mother's teats, taking their morning meal. The mare's stood unmoving, seeming almost oblivious of the colt's actions, while their alert eyes moved over the land looking for danger. The young mares without colts were grazing, having decided to let the old mares keep lookout.

Charlie waited for the colts to finish before he made his presence known. He knew the colts were old enough to survive on grass alone; still the rich milk was a fine breakfast for them.

He held the lariat, the open loop in his right hand and the remaining length coiled in the other hand. He had practiced scores of times with the lariat and had become very skilled at dropping the loop over the animal he intended to catch. He hoped the mares would be sufficiently used to humans, having been branded with the Wolf Trap brand and most likely herded about for other reasons, and would not spook at the first sight of him. The colts would soon be branded and that was why he must accomplish his thievery now before that happened.

One after another the colts finish nursing, and as they did so their dams began to graze the grass. When the last colt stopped nursing and lifted its head and looked about, Charlie walked slowly into the meadow. His throwing arm was cocked to hurl the open noose.

One mare spotted Charlie and snorted an alarm. The remaining mares, alerted by the snort, quickly turned to face Charlie. The colts copied their dams, coming to a rigid and watchful stance with eyes fixed on the man.

"Easy, ladies. Easy, ladies." Charlie called out in a low and gentle voice to the horses as he approached them.

All stood tense, their large brown eyes wide and pointed ears cocked toward Charlie. As he drew closer, the nearest mare, a beautiful roan, stomped the ground and her tail switched nervously. She looked ready to run and he must make his choice quickly.

Charlie wanted a female colt and hastily scanned the youngsters. A black filly colt, with her right front leg wearing a white stocking, had stepped out in front of her dam. Filled with curiosity, she was totally fixed upon him. He was captivated by the elegant creature, the arch of her neck, the length of her back, and above all the clear liquid brown oval of her keen, inquisitive eyes.

"You're the one, little girl." Charlie had now moved within range of his lariat. He flung the loop, sending it shooting through the air.

The colt saw the loop of the lariat streaking toward it. She dodged to the side. But too late. The loop settled over her head and around her neck.

Charlie jerked the lariat and closed the noose around the lovely neck. The herd of mares and the remaining colts stampeded away. The little filly whirled to follow and was jerked up short, almost losing her footing on the end of the lariat. She gathered herself together and leapt away, only to be halted in mid-stride and to fall. She scrambled to her feet and fought the lariat, rearing and thrashing her hooves in the air. Charlie had come swiftly down the lariat hand over hand and now wrapped the colt in his arms and held her pressed tightly against him.

"Easy, little lady. Nobody'll hurt you. Now you and I must get to know each other for we will have many years together and you will give me beautiful colts. That is unless I get caught and hung." Charlie laughed without humor. This was colt number eighteen he had stolen from Coldiron.

"But he must catch me first," he said, rubbing the colt's head and enjoying the fine velvet feel of her hair and skin. He leaned and blew into the colt's face several times. "Remember my smell so that you will know me even in the darkest night and not be afraid."

He squatted beside the filly, and reaching under her, captured her legs with his arms and pulled them from under her and laid her down on her side. He straddled her and held her thrashing body penned. He removed the pack from his shoulders and dug out four thick pieces of the burlap similar to that which he wore, but much smaller. These he tied around the colt's hooves. He placed a lead rope around her neck and removed the lariat.

"Let's travel, little girl, before somebody sees me and I get in big trouble."

Charlie rose and the colt immediately sprang to her feet. Towing the resisting and struggling colt that was trying to follow her mother, he struck out with a swift pace toward the stone fence that he had climbed over to enter Coldiron's domain. After a short distance, the little filly gave up the battle against the man and trotted to keep up.

At the fence, Charlie removed half a dozen slabs of the stone, and then pulled on the lead line to force the filly to jump over the remaining barrier. One of her front hooves caught on the edge of a stone and she stumbled, but with her youthful quickness caught herself and landed on her feet.

Charlie relayed the stones, being careful to make the wall appear as it had before. He did not want the implacable Luke Coldiron, or his Ute Indian wranglers to discover the loss of the colt and come chasing him.

He hurried away to the southwest with his stolen prize. Always, he avoided the meadows and chose the hard and rocky ground so as to leave no trace of the colt and his passing. He kept notice of the burlap as it wore away, and twice renewed the burlap on his and the colt's feet. Often he scanned ahead down over the rolling foothills hazy with distance and pressed down by the sapphire-blue bowl of the morning sky. Beyond his vision and nearly thirty miles away lay Santa Fe, his destination. He would make one stop before Santa Fe.

***

Charlie found his horse grazing where he had left it in the opening in the pine woods. It lifted its head and nickered a welcoming greeting to him. The horse's action told Charlie that they were alone in the woods and this made him feel more secure and he hurried onward to the animal.

He knelt beside the colt. The burlap had worn through on the colt's hooves, and also on his feet. He removed all the remnants and hid them under a large, flat rock. He led the colt to the live stream of water coming from the spring at the base of a low outcropping of lava. The colt eagerly lowered her head and drank with a soft sucking sound. Charlie lay down and drank beside her, the cold water a fine feeling sliding down his throat. He filled his canteen and rose.

He went to the horse and removed its hobbles and tightened the saddle girth. His pack was tied behind the saddle and he mounted. Leading the colt, he rode out of the clearing and continued the long trek down through the foothills of the mountain.

He felt ever greater relief as he put distance between himself and Coldiron's land. Yet at the same time with every mile made good, he was drawing closer to Santa Fe and that meant the chances were growing that he would encounter other men. Should they see him with the fine colt, they might ask where he had gotten it, or perhaps even ask to buy it. Worse, they could recognize a Coldiron colt and notify the owner and identify the person who had the animal.

He stopped every hour or so to allow the little filly to rest. She was used to traveling, but not for miles on end. The first few times they halted, she simply stood quietly. Then as the day grew long and the miles added up, she began to lie down during the periods of rest.

The pine forest fell away behind as the elevation decreased and junipers dotted the land. Shortly thereafter he came upon the road connecting Santa Fe with Taos to the north. He looked both ways along the much traveled way. Finding the road empty, he speedily crossed it and continued on into the woods until out of sight of any travelers. There he turned south with the road off on his left and the Rio Grande, flowing in its two hundred foot lava rimmed gorge, some two miles away on his right.

Once as he journeyed, he saw a horseman silhouetted on a hill top ahead. He hastily pulled back out of view. Another time, he saw two woodcutters swinging axes as they chopped wood, their six burros standing close by and waiting to be loaded. He detoured around them. A mile later, he climbed to the top of a hill holding a few scattered junipers, and their dismounted.

He looked to the south toward Santa Fe. In the warming afternoon with its updrafts, a great towering thunderhead was building over the land; its crown was rising, boiling up ever higher in large white billows. The thunderhead's bottom was dark gray and swollen with the huge quantity of moisture it held. From Charlie's position, the thunderhead appeared to hang over Santa Fe and the surrounding area. He hoped it would rain for the land was dry and needed a soaking.

Charlie sat down on the ground. He would wait for night and darkness before continuing on. The colt lay down wearily beside him. It placed its head on its front legs and sighed with weariness. Charlie smiled at the colt's sigh, so much like a sound a tired human might make. He reached out and stroked the animal, the sunlight from the low hanging sun made its sleek black coat glisten.

He sat quietly and watched the sun roll down the last of its ancient sky path to the horizon and turn the puffs of clouds that lay there into clots of dark scarlet, the color of old blood. Like the blood he had seen too much of in the battles in Mexico. He forced his mind away from that time for it was not good to remember such things. He continued to stroke the colt, and considering what the future might bring for the two of them. As he did so, time continued to tick away and the sun fell ever more and the day weakened to gray dusk.

Charlie rose and tugged on the lead rope. The colt came to her feet, but stood staggering.

"I understand, little lady. It's your turn to ride and for me to walk." The colt had traveled many miles and

Charlie was pleased with her stamina. That predicted a strong mare when fully grown. Perhaps he would train her to be his riding horse.

He removed the pack and fastened it across the saddle. He then tied the front legs of the colt together, and then the rear ones together. Catching the one hundred and fifty pound animal up in his arms, he laid her across the rump of the horse just behind the saddle, and tied her there. That position would provide her with a much more comfortable ride than the hard saddle made for a man to straddle. He continued his journey leading his horse.

***

The night came and fell upon the land. The shroud of darkness congealed quickly; to Charlie it seemed to have weight, substance. He had been out in the night many times in his eighteen years of life and never had he seen such blackness. He reached out a hand and moved it back and forth through the darkness. And felt nothing. A strange and unexpected emotion came over him. He recalled the blood color of the sunset and now the extraordinarily black night. Were the events somehow a warning of danger ahead? Stealing the colt was but part of his plan, with many equally perilous actions yet to accomplish and each one would be an opportunity for things to go badly.

He shook his head in the blackness and shoved the thoughts of omens away. He veered to the left until he found the road and continued along it. In the dark there was little likely hood that he would meet anyone traveling. Even if he should, they would not be able to identify him or what he had tied to the back of his horse.

He was drawing ever nearer to his first destination and now and again encountered a house along the road. He walked on until at last he saw the yellow square of candlelight in the window of the house he sought. He left the road and approached the house, to halt under the aged apple tree by the rail fence that protected the garden from the owner's sheep.

He tied the reins of his horse to a fence post. Gently he unloaded the colt and removed the cords that bound her legs. She immediately lay down. He fastened her lead rope to the fence.

He faced the house. The structure was but a dark outline in the night, but he knew it well, an adobe house of smallish size sitting a quarter mile away from the steep bank of the Rio Grande. Were the people he expected to be there alone, or were others there? No use to wonder. He moved stealthily to the window and peered inside.

***

Perla Armentes sat at the table with her brother Ernesto. They did not speak, they simply waited. She knew Ernesto's friend, Charlie Bell, would soon arrive, as he had done several nights over the past two months. Ernesto was tapping the table nervously and she wished mightily to know why he was so on edge at these particular times. What was really happening?

She had done all that could be done to prepare for their visitor. The house with its two bedrooms, sitting room and kitchen was spotless. She had bathed and donned her pretty blue dress. Her hair was combed and tied behind her head with a blue ribbon that matched her dress.

A knock sounded on the door and her pulse quickened. She quickly came to her feet. Ernesto rose also, and limping but slightly, hastened across the room and opened the door.

Charlie entered, bending forward to pass under the door frame. Ernesto, with a questioning expression, looked up at Charlie, who nodded. Ernesto nodded back, took his hat from the peg on the wall near the door and left, closing the door behind him.

Perla had noted the silent communication between the two men and anger flared through her, as it had at all the other times. She was angry at both of them for the secret they kept from her. She had asked Ernesto why she could not be part of it. He had replied that the reason was very simple; she was a blabber-mouth who told all that she knew to her girlfriends. Perla knew there was some truth in that, however she would watch them very closely and would find out what the two were doing that required so much secrecy. She focused on Charlie and her anger vanished.

He had removed his hat and was steadily observing her with his blue eyes that told nothing of what he was thinking. He was the tallest man she had ever known. She ran her sight over his blond hair and his sharply chiseled face with the nose straight and high and the forehead broad. He was not a handsome man, she judged, at least not in the way Mexican men were with their black hair and dark eyes. Then he smiled that big smile he had that softened the angularity of his face, and to her, yes he was handsome.

"Hello, Perla," he said with that slow measured way he had of speaking.

"Hello, Charlie." Perla could not but smile back happily at the sound of her name upon this man's lips. "Are you hungry?"

"A better word would be starved."

"Then wash up while I set a place for you. I've kept your food warm on the stove. Ernesto and I ate earlier."

"Thank you," Charlie said. He hung his hat on the peg that had held Ernesto's, and his holstered pistol on a second one. He turned to the wash basin close by on its stand. The basin was full of fresh water and a clean towel hung ready for drying his face and hands. All this, the food ready and warm and this thoughtfulness with the water in the basin, she had done for him. He looked at her and smiled gently.

He washed his hands and face, ran his wet fingers through his hair to position it to hide the scar on his skull. He didn't want people to see the scar. Especially Perla.

He turned and watched Perla hastening to set out his meal. He noted, as he had many times before, that she was already womanly rounded at sixteen, breast and hips pressing and bulging the cloth of her dress. Her hair was thick and black, skin a dusky silk. He felt that urge that always came to him to touch the smooth brown curve of her cheek, and other places.

"Please be seated," Perla said, indicating the chair with her hand.

As Charlie seated himself, Perla sat down across the small table opposite him. He had a huge appetite and she liked to see him eat the food she had prepared for him.

"It looks great," Charlie said as he ladled out a large portion of the soup containing several kinds of vegetables. He cut a big wedge of bread from the loaf still in its pan and added it to his plate. Three quarters of a thick crusted apple pie and a large mug of black coffee promised a grand addition to the meal. His sweet tooth would be fed. He began to eat, savoring the delightful taste that his deep hunger added to the food. He glanced at Perla. She too with her prettiness and friendliness added flavor to the food.

Perla remained silent as Charlie ate. Now and again he glanced at her with that penetrating way he had. What was he thinking? She wished he would talk with her; tell her of some of his thoughts.

Finally he laid his fork and spoon in his plate and took up the coffee mug. One of his hands rested on the table near Perla. She reached out and clasped it with both of hers.

"Charlie, tell me what you and Ernesto are doing that's so secret," Perla said.

"I can't. I promised Ernesto that I wouldn't."

"But I would keep it a secret." Perla knew a strong friendship existed between the two men. They had appeared at the house a year and a half ago, two bearded, gaunt young men wearing pistols and riding on horseback. Ernesto limped from a wound. The tall American appeared unhurt. Ernesto had been changed so much that Perla had barely recognized him at first glance. She had prayed for his safe return and was much gladdened to see him.

She told her brother of the death of their father, how he had fallen into the deep gorge of the Rio Grande. How one of the sheep had found its way onto a rock ledge part way down into the gorge and her father had tried to rescue it and lost his footing and fell. The news of the death greatly saddened Ernesto.

He had introduced Charlie and said he would stay a few days with them. Charlie had spent but the night and early the following morning left for Santa Fe. She had not again seen him for several days. Recently they had begun this secret thing that they kept from her.

"I believe you would, but I must keep my word to Ernesto."

"Please tell me."

Charlie shook his head.

"You know there is one secret that I've been keeping." Perla said, her brash eyes sparking mischievously.

Charlie smiled his huge smile at her words. "Yes, I know you are."

He stood up and Perla stood up beside him. He scooped her up in his arms and pulled her tightly to him.

Perla gave a small moan of pleasure at the touch of him, the feel of his muscular body against her. She pressed her cheek against his neck and felt the powerful pulse in his jugular. She liked the size of him immensely. She breathed in the odor of him, and caught the scent of the resin of pines trees of the forest, and the smell of dust and a bit of horse. She smile to herself, he had not been in Santa Fe to see a girl.

Charlie carried Perla across the room and into her bedroom where he placed her on the bed. She immediately came into his arms and he kissed her and hugged her close. Her breath came faster as she anticipated what was to come next.

Charlie laughed, pulled free and began to remove his clothing.

"Hurry," Perla whispered.

Charlie almost laughed out loud. He much enjoyed Perla's eagerness for the love making.

Charlie left the Armente's home an hour later, mounted his horse and rode through the darkness toward Santa Fe.

Chapter Thirteen

Luke Coldiron entered Santa Fe along San Francisco Street. He was mounted upon his favorite horse, a black mare with a soft step and a rocking chair lope. He had ridden for six hours down from his ranch in the mountains to the town and was anticipating drinking a beer, or more likely two. Then a bath to remove the dust of the journey, and when the night came, he would visit a certain pretty woman.

Luke had made enemies over the years and wore a holstered pistol strapped to his side and a rifle in a scabbard under his left leg. Since the end of the war, there had been a large increase in the town's population. Most of the newcomers were honest and earned their living by hard work. Then there were the crooked men, the robbers and thieves and head bashers who preyed upon the honest ones. To add to the Luke's danger, somewhat more than a year past, three men had stolen some of his horses and he had chased them down and shot them. Their friends, if they had any, might take revenge should the opportunity present itself. He would be wary; still he planned to enjoy the pleasures of the town.

He looked along San Francisco Street lined with adobe and stone buildings one and two stories tall. The street led directly to the central plaza of the town. Most of the structures were jammed tightly against their neighbors and often had a common wall between them. The street and the plaza taken together made the business center of the town, containing all types of activity, general stores, restaurants, gunsmiths, blacksmiths, a funeral parlor and saloons, a few were also brothels.

Scores of people on private errands moved along the street. A pair of American soldiers carrying muskets, one of the army's roving patrols that guarded and policed the city, stood on a corner and watched for troublemakers. Four traders' wagons were parked in front of a warehouse. Men were unloading cargo; boxes, crates, barrels and bulging sacks from the wagons and carrying them inside the building. Luke judged that the traders were recent arrivals along the nine hundred mile Santa Fe Trail from Independence, Missouri. At the hitching rails of the stores, offices, and drinking and eating establishment, nearly a hundred saddled horses stood heads down, half asleep in the mild autumn evening.

Luke reached the end of the street and came out onto the broad central plaza of the town. On the north side was the Palace of the Governors. For many decades it had been occupied by the Mexican governor. On August

21, 1846, at the beginning of the Mexican-American War, General Kearny had occupied Santa Fe and had made the palace his headquarters. All of the subsequent American governors had followed his lead. Currently it was occupied by the American Territorial Governor, Colonel John Munroe. His thousand troopers were billeted in Fort Marcy, a large adobe and brick structure built on a hill close-by, overlooking the town.

In the lengthening evening shadows, the big plaza was bustling with men, women and children. Standing out from all the other people were two bearded men in fringed buckskin. No rifle or pistol was in sight; however each man carried a long-bladed skinning knife in a sheath on his belt. Luke recognized the kind of men they were, mountain trappers. He had once, years in the past, been one of them. Back then, there would have been two dozen or more of such men in Santa Fe at this time of year and getting outfitted for the winter's trapping in the high mountains to the north. Now fur trapping was almost a thing of the past.

On his left side, and leaning against the front of a dry goods store, were three Mexican vaqueros, Mexican cowboys, in tightly fitting leather pants, intricately decorated jackets, leather boots and large-brimmed hats with high peaked crowns. All three were unarmed, as the American military had ordered. They stared with unfriendly eyes at Luke for a moment and then looked away.

Two young and pretty dark skinned senoritas with rouged cheeks and lips and wearing brightly colored dresses, walked with lovely swinging strides toward the central plaza. They smiled at Luke, telling him that they thought him a handsome fellow. The taller one winked at him. He could not help but smile back, remembering something an old trapper friend of years past, had once said, "If God had created anything more beautiful than a young woman, God had kept it for himself."

He guided the mare toward La Fonda, a building on the corner of the plaza. La Fonda was a hotel, restaurant, saloon and gambling parlor. The best food and lodging in town were found there. As he drew close to La Fonda, he saw a woodcutter unloading wood from his burro at the rear of the building. Andy, a lad of ten that Luke knew, was carrying the wood toward the woodshed at the back of La Fonda.

"Luke, Luke Coldiron, wait up," a man called from off on Luke's right.

Luke halted and looked in the direction of the voice. Colonel Munroe was coming toward him with his usual military stride. The colonel raised a hand in greeting.

Luke returned the gesture and reined in his mount. "Hello, colonel."

The officer came up and stopped. "Luke, I'd like to have a few words with you if you have some time."

"Sure. I've got time."

"Would you come to my office?" The colonel gestured at the Governors Palace.

"Colonel, I've had a long ride and I'm thirsty so let's have a beer at La Fonda while we talk."

The colonel nodded quick agreement. "That would be fine for I could use a drink."

Luke rode onward toward La Fonda, with the colonel walking along beside Luke and his horse.

Luke liked the colonel. He had proven himself to General Zachary Taylor in the war in northern Mexico, especially the hard fought battle against General Santa Ana at Monterrey. That had led to his appointment as territorial governor by President Zachary Taylor, who had become president upon President Polk's death. Munroe was a tall, angular Scotsman. He had a bulldog face that made him one of the ugliest men Luke had ever seen. His full beard did little to hide that ugliness, Luke thought. He knew that behind that unsightly face was a very keen mind. He also knew that the man had a bad temper in the morning before he relaxed with strong drink around noon. Even afterwards, he still had a hard, no-nonsense manner about him. Luke thought the colonel might be too hard.

Luke halted at La Fonda, dismounted and tied his mare with the half score horses at the hitching rail. He and the colonel entered the wide entrance of La Fonda side by side.

From many previous days spent at La Fonda, Luke knew that on the right hand side past a short expanse of wall was a quite large saloon with many tables and a long mahogany bar. Part of the saloon was set aside for gambling. Directly ahead past the saloon, a wide hallway led to the hotel and restaurant portion of La Fonda. Beyond the hotel was the bathhouse, and further back yet and out a rear door, was an interior courtyard, and beyond that, a walled corral for the horses of the patrons of the hotel.

Luke and the colonel entered the saloon, a wide space with a high ceiling from which hung a huge chandelier. Of the dozen or so tables, only one was being used, four men were talking over a map spread before them.

Luke and the colonel took a seat at a distance from the men. Luke called out to the bartender who had come out from behind the bar and was coming toward them.

"Two large, cold ones," Luke called out.

The bartender nodded and retreated back to the bar and began to fill the mugs.

"It's good to see you, Luke," said the colonel. "You should come to town more often."

"I agree. But it seems that there is always something that needs to be done at the ranch."

"Your ranch is in Ute country. Any trouble from them?"

"No. I have two of their young men working for me and that keeps everybody happy. They're names are Thunder Hawk and Jumping Eagle."

"They good workers?"

"They're a little wild, especially Jumping Eagle the youngest. But damn fine horse wranglers and good trackers too. If they ever get into trouble here in Santa Fe, I hope you'll go easy on them. Any trouble will be started by the bully boys here in town that don't like Indians."

"I'll remember that."

The bartender came up and sat the beers before the two men. Luke handed the man coins in payment and he left.

Luke picked up his mug and took a drink of the first brew he had had in weeks. He held it in his mouth for a few seconds, savoring its taste and coolness before swallowing it.

The colonel drank half of his beer in one long upending pull from his mug.

Luke caught movement out of the corner of his eye and turned to see a man had come into view from the hallway leading to the rear of La Fonda. From the man's clothing, Luke judged him to be a Texan. He was buckling a holstered pistol and a knife in a sheath around his waist. He cast a glance into the saloon as he continued on toward the exit.

A boy's voice came from the hallway leading to the rear part of La Fonda. "Mister, you forgot to pay me."

The man, seemingly not hearing the boy's call, kept on toward the entrance.

Andy, the boy who tended the baths, came hurrying into sight and up behind the man. He called out, "Mister, you owe me twenty cents for the bath water I brought you!"

"Go away, kid," the man growled over his shoulder.

"Mister, you used four buckets of water and that counts to twenty cents at five cents a bucket."

"The damn water was cold and I don't pay for cold bath water."

"It was plenty hot, just like I always heat it. And you owe me." Andy reached out and caught the man by the arm.

The man jerked his arm free. "Get away from me you little bastard before I slap you damn face." The man raised his hand in a threatening manner.

Anger surged through Luke and he leapt to his feet. The boy would not be struck and he would be paid.

As Luke was about to shout out for the cheat to pay, Charlie Bell came into view with swift steps from the entrance of La Fonda. He halted close in front of the cheat and spoke in a firm voice. "I heard what Andy said about the water. He always heats the water plenty hot for a bath. You should pay him."

"I don't know why this is any of your damn business, but the water was cold."

"Charlie, the water was plenty hot, just like I heat it for you," Andy said.

"It was cold. Now get out of my way." He made to move past Charlie.

"Hold up," Charlie said and put up a hand. "Let's not argue about the water for it's too late to tell if it was hot or cold. But you owe me and I want paid. Do you plan to pay me?"

"Hell yes. That's different."

"That's good. Your horse is tied up out front. I removed the horse shoes, trimmed the hooves and nailed the shoes back on just as you wanted. That'll be two dollars and twenty cents."

"You mean two dollars. That's the price the blacksmith always charges. Fifty cents a hoof."

"Today I did the work and the price is two dollars and twenty cents." Charlie held out his hand with the palm up.

"I'll not pay but two dollars. I'll go see Ferguson. Now get out of the way."

"Not until you pay me. Then you can do whatever you want."

"Get out of my way before you get hurt," said the man. He backed up a step and dropped his hand to the butt of his pistol.

With two swift steps, Charlie was upon the man and his left hand shot out and caught hold of the pistol as it came free of the holster. Charlie's right hand swept up and clamped the man around the neck, tumbling the hat from his head. He rammed him backward two steps and slammed him into the wall. The wall shook and the big chandelier hanging on its chain in the saloon jerked and rattled.

"Any man who touched his gun means to hurt somebody. Today that somebody might be me." Charlie wrenched the pistol from the man's hand and sent it skittering away across the floor.

"Damn you." The man struck at Charlie.

Charlie blocked the fist with his elbow. He drew the man away from the wall and slammed him into it.

"You try that again and I'll break your damn neck." He closed his hand more tightly around the man's neck. "Now do I get paid two dollars and twenty cents or do I get rough with you?"

"I'll pay," gasped the man.

Charlie removed both hands from the man's neck and stepped back. "Then we have no disagreement." He held out his hand.

The man, trembling with rage, dug into a pants pocket and brought out a handful of coins. He selected two silver dollars and two dimes and slapped them down upon Charlie's hand.

"Thanks," said Charlie.

Ignoring the man's red faced anger, Charlie turned to Andy. He smiled at the boy. "A man should always be paid for his work. Here, Andy, catch."

He flipped a dime, and then a second one. The boy nimbly caught each tumbling coin out of the air.

"Charlie, the water was plenty warm," Andy said.

"I'm sure it was," Charlie replied.

He turned to leave La Fonda, and as he did so, he looked into the saloon. Watching him intently were Luke Coldiron and Colonel Munroe. The colonel was the law in New Mexico and hung horse thieves. Coldiron also hung horse thieves. Charlie's breath caught. He quickened his pace toward the door from La Fonda.

Luke was about to get back to his beer when he caught movement from the would-be cheat. The man had pulled a knife from its sheath and was moving up behind

Charlie. As he lifted it to strike at Charlie's departing back, Luke drew his pistol and fired.

The man flinched at the explosion of the pistol and the deadly snarl of the bullet barely missing the bridge of his nose. He froze.

Charlie whirled at the boom of the pistol behind him, and seeing the knife in the startled man's hand, rushed upon him and ripped it from his grip. He swung his right fist, crashing it into the side of the man's face, snapping his head to the side. The man fell slack and unconscious.

Charlie turned to look into the saloon. Coldiron held a pistol and a cloud of gun smoke was rising toward the ceiling. Charlie understood Coldiron had been the one who had fired a pistol. That shot had stopped the man from stabbing Charlie.

"Thanks," Charlie called out. "That's one I owe you."

"He just needed a reminder not to knife a man in the back," Luke replied, liking the young fellow.

Charlie switched worried eyes to the colonel. "Am I in any trouble, colonel?"

"None. You did what had to be done. I'll take care of that fellow."

Charlie dropped the man's knife down beside his unconscious body and hastily left La Fonda. His mind raced with what had just happened and Coldiron's part in it.

207

Damnation! The man whose colts he had stolen had just saved him from being knifed. With that troubling knowledge, he made his way across the plaza in the direction of the blacksmith shop.

***

"Luke, you should have killed that man," the colonel said in a reproachful tone.

"I considered doing just that", Luke said. "But then decided you might not like it."

"Hell. I would have sworn that shooting him was necessary to save a life. And it would've helped me solve a problem that I've got. Now you have made an enemy of someone who would kill an unarmed man. And so does that young fellow." The colonel paused, and then asked, "By the way, who is he?"

"His name's Charlie Bell," Luke replied. "He works for Ferguson the blacksmith. Ferguson said he was a damn good one too."

"He's strong and quick and would make a good soldier. And the army always needs a good blacksmith. I'll have my recruiting officer talk with him about enlisting."

"Might work."

A stomp of running feet sounded at the entrance of La Fonda and two soldiers of Colonel Munroe's roving patrol came hurrying into view. They halted at sight of Munroe. The men hastily saluted.

"We heard a shot," said the corporal of the patrol in explanation for presence.

"It's good you're here," replied the colonel. He gestured at the man lying and groaning on the floor. "Take that fellow out of here."

"Should I lock him up, colonel?"

Munroe considered the question. He didn't want to waste time holding a hearing on the fellow. "No. He's had enough punishment this time. Just dump him on the sidewalk."

"Yes, sir." Each soldier grabbed an arm of the man and dragged him from La Fonda.

"You said you wanted to talk about something special," Luke prompted the colonel.

"Yes, and that man they just took out of here is part of it. His name is Kassor and he works for a man named Max Cleland. This Cleland is a Texan and a Mexican hater and was one of the men who helped pay for that Texas invasion of New Mexico back in 1841."

Luke smiled. "Yeah, the Texas army that got lost on the Staked Plains and ran out of water and food. Then got captured by the Mexican army without a fight."

"The very same. Cleland is here in New Mexico and he's brought eight tough looking men with him. Though

Kassor didn't seem too tough in Bell's hands. Anyway, Cleland is buying up much Mexican owned land near Socorro."

"That's a problem?"

"It's all right for him to do that except I've heard that he's paying only a few cents on the peso for it. I want to know how he's getting away with that."

"You've tried to find out, I'm sure."

"Yes. I sent an officer down there. The people who sold their land have all gone to old Mexico. And their friends wouldn't talk to my man."

"Was he in uniform?"

"I know what you're thinking, that they wouldn't talk with a soldier, not after so many Mexicans were killed during the war. That's why I'm asking a favor. You have many friends among the Mexicans. Would you find out what's going on with the land sales? The treaty we made with the Mexican Government plainly states that every Mexican can keep ownership of his land. I have strict orders to enforce that provision."

"That sounds fair to me." said Luke. "Some of these people have owned land for generations."

"I asked a friend of mine stationed at the Army head-quarters in Houston about Cleland. He told me Cleland owns land and other businesses in Texas. And that he is a personal friend of Sam Houston."

"Does that make a difference," Luke asked.

Munroe gave Luke a quick look. "Not to me. If he's done something to break the treaty, I'll arrest him and send him to Washington and let President and the army generals deal with him."

"I'm going to Socorro tomorrow with horses I've sold to Pedro Armendaris. He owns a big rancho there and will know what's going on. I'll ask him."

"Thanks. Let's have another beer. I'll pay."

"That's a fair offer."

***

Luke lay soaking in warm water in one of the bathing room of La Fonda. As Andy poured the last bucket of water into the tub, Luke spoke to the boy. "Andy, do you know the woman that owns the Donnelly dress shop on San Francisco Street?"

"I sure do, Mr. Coldiron. She once made me a pair of pants real cheap"

"I thought you might. There's a dime in it if you will take a message to her. It's that piece of paper lying on the table there near my clothes. She'll give you a message to bring back to me." The answer to the note was very important to Luke for it could decide how much enjoyment the evening would hold for him.

"I'll do it right now." Andy swiftly grabbed up the paper and scooted out the door.

Luke's heart increased its beat as the memory of his first sight of beautiful Liza Donnelly came to him. He had been in San Santa Fe in the spring when the first caravan of merchant's wagons, containing sixteen wagons, and the heavily armed horsemen who guarded the cargo from robbers and Indians, arrived from Independence, Missouri. As they always did, the merchants drove their big heavily laden wagons, each wagon pulled by two teams of horses, through the main plaza to announce their presence to the town. Luke and two score of business men and ordinary citizens had followed the caravan from the plaza to San Francisco Street. The freighters would have the latest newspapers, and other news, from the eastern part of the nation.

The caravan had halted on the street. The freighters, and those people who had purchased transportation to Santa Fe, climbed down from their wagon seats and the horsemen from their mounts. Luke had been much surprised when he saw a slender woman dressed in sturdy men's clothing climb down from a wagon. He wondered how she came to be among the men.

She looked out from under the broad brim of her hat at the throng of people staring at the new arrivals, and then turned to survey the several businesses fronting the street. She smiled, and to Luke the smile seemed one of much satisfaction at being in Santa Fe.

She called out to two sturdy young men of the town who stood not far away and asked if they would help her unload her possessions from the wagon. Smiling broadly, they readily agreed. At her direction they lifted down from the wagon and placed on the sidewalk a large box, a sewing machine, a bulging suitcase and a smaller one, and something large and bulky wrapped in canvas. Luke would learn later the bulky parcel was several rolls of different types and colors of cloth.

Luke moved closer for a better view of the woman. He judged her to be about thirty years of age. Her eyes were large and brown. Her skin, which must surely have been quite fair when she had left on the nine hundred mile journey from Missouri, was now burnished from forty days of travel under the sun, wind and rain with which the prairie and the mountains always greeted travelers. Her mouth was of perfect proportions and she possessed a fine straight nose. Her hair was dark brown. Luke finished his evaluation of the woman and knowing he had made a fine discovery.

The woman asked the two young fellows to stand guard over her possession. She then hastened away, and in a few minutes had found a place for a fee to store her belongings at the general store close-by. The fellows carried the items to the storeroom at the rear of the store. When she offered to pay the two, they refused, each giving the woman a broad smile and then walking away casting glances back over their shoulders at her.

The woman saw Luke watching her and she smiled and spoke to him. "You look like you might know the town. Where is the nearest hotel?"

"There are two in that direction just a short ways," Luke replied and pointed along the street. "La Fonda on the plaza is the best. Then there is a smaller one just this side of the plaza. May I show you where they are?"

"Yes, thank you." She picked up her suitcase and fell in beside Luke and they moved off along the street.

Luke considered offering to carry the suitcase, but there was something about the way she had picked it up and now carried it, that told him not to.

They walked a few steps and Luke spoke. "My name is Luke Coldiron," He wanted to find out who she was, and why she was in Santa Fe.

"I'm Mrs. Liza Donnelly,"

"You're from Missouri, I would guess," Luke said and wondering where the husband was.

"Yes, from Independence."

"You'll find it different here."

"I Imagine I will. But that's all right."

They had drawn near the small hotel and Liza spoke. "Have you ever stayed at this hotel?"

"No. I always stay at La Fonda."

"Well, I'll take a gamble that this one is reasonably clean. Thank you, Mr. Coldiron, for guiding me." She held out her hand, and that surprised Luke for women rarely shook hands with a man. At least not offering hers first.

He quickly caught her hand and pressed it gently, enjoying the feel of the warm skin and flesh covering the fine bones within. It was a pleasure just to touch Liza Donnelly.

"La Fonda has the best food in town," Luke said, still holding Liza's hand.

"I'll remember that," Liza said and extracted her hand from Luke's. She smiled at him, turned away and entered the hotel.

Luke saw Liza again three days later when he came to San Francisco Street to have a saddle repaired at O'Fallon's saddle shop. He was much surprise at what he found. She had rented an empty building of modest size, wedged in between two larger buildings, just off the plaza, and had renovated the space for a business. A painter was hanging a sign over the entrance. The sign read in black letters on a white background, Mrs. Liza

Donnelly, Tailor and Seamstress, Maker Of Fine Clothing.

As Luke drew closer to get a better view of what Liza had accomplished, the painter climbed down from his ladder. He called into the building and Liza came outside dressed in a man's shirt and trousers. Luke noted white paint stains on her hands. She stood on the sidewalk and evaluated the sign.

"Well done, Mr. Conners." Liza said. She removed money from a shirt pocket and counted part of it out to Conners.

"Thank you, mam," the man said and bobbed his head in acknowledgement of the compliment and payment. He took up his ladder and went off along the street.

Liza, appearing pleased with what she had accomplished, reentered her place of business. A moment later, she hung a sign, Open For Business, in the front window.

"I'll be damned," Luke said to himself.

He had gone into the shop and immediately ordered a complete outfit of clothing from the skin out to get Liza Donnelly's business off to a successful start. She had measured him for the suit with the skill of a professional tailor. When he had commented on that, she had told him that she and her husband had owned and operated a tailor shop in Independence for eight years before his death from cholera. She had decided to come to Santa Fe to try her fortune in a place far away from Independence. She ended the conversation by promising the suit would be ready in two days.

Late that night, Luke cashed out of a game of poker and came out onto San Francisco Street stretching left and right, dark and deserted. He had won some money, but nothing to brag about. Sleep was hovering about the edges of his mind and he moved off toward his bed at La Fonda, its location marked by a distant point of light from an oil burning street lamp on the main plaza of the town.

Luke's course took him past Liza's shop, and, to his surprise, lamplight shone around the edges of the blind drawn over the front window. He halted and peered past the edge of the blind and into the store. Liza sat leaning over her sewing machine, her foot pumping the treadle that propelled the machine, the needle stabbing up and down as it sewed a stitch in the black wool cloth Luke had selected for his suit. Greatly impressed by Liza's willingness to work long hours to be successful in her new business, Luke pulled back from his stolen look at her and went off along the street. He smiled to himself.

Two days after ordering his suit, Luke appeared at the shop to pick up the garments. Liza greeted him pleasantly and directed him to try the clothing on behind a curtain that closed off a small section of the rear of the shop. Dressed in his new suit, that fit perfectly, Luke had asked Liza to have dinner with him at La Fonda.

He was surprised at her answer and remembered every word, "I knew you would ask me and I have been considering what I would say. The answer is yes, Mr. Coldiron, I would be delighted to have dinner with you."

Now with thoughts of the pleasures of the coming evening, Luke had completed his bath and was dressed in the finely tailored suit created by Liza when Andy returned.

The boy was smiling hugely as he handed Luke a folded piece of paper. "Here's Mrs. Donnelly note. She sure is pretty."

"That she is," Luke replied as he took the paper. He read – Mr. Coldiron, I would be most pleased to see you at seven this evening for dinner at my home. Liza.

"Good news, Mr. Coldiron?"

"Don't you know?"

Andy grinned hugely.

Luke dug into a pocket and handed Andy a dime. And then a second one.

"Good news is worth double payment."

"Wow. Thanks, Mr. Coldiron." Smiling broadly, Andy hurried away.

Luke checked his pocket watch. Two long hours to wait.

Chapter Fourteen

In the long shadows of the evening, Luke strolled leisurely along the wooden sidewalk and among the people on San Francisco Street. He still had half an hour remaining before he was due at Liza Donnelly's home, and had decided to walk there. After spending so much of his time in the mountains, he enjoyed watching the townsfolk going about on their private errands and hearing their voices in conversation.

He moved aside for a man and his woman walking side by side. The man nodded a 'thanks' as he passed. A few steps later, Luke halted abruptly so as not to step on two small girls racing past in a game of 'tag'. Their laughing childish voices added to his already high spirits. He admitted to himself that he liked people, at least most of them. Sometimes he was lonely in the mountains. Perhaps he should consider taking a woman home with him from one of his trips to town. There were plenty of them in Santa Fe. Why not Liza? He would give that serious thought.

He continued on and shortly left the section of San Francisco Street that catered to the common folk and their businesses, and entered the rough section of town with its saloons, gambling parlors, whorehouses and the hangouts of the toughs of the town.

He came to The Independence, the largest saloon and whorehouse in Santa Fe. The sound of the music of a piano and banjo playing together came through the open door and out onto the street. He thought that was an odd combination of musical instruments. He glanced through the big front window to the interior of the saloon. It was crowded with patrons - soldiers in uniforms, cattlemen with their hats and boots, lumbermen in their coarse clothing, townsmen, and the women who serviced the men in all ways.

As Luke continued onward, Kassor came out through the entrance of the saloon. He was accompanied by a rail thin man that Luke had never seen before. Kassor caught sight of Luke approaching and his face tightened with sudden anger. He spoke to the man with him. The man said something in reply. Something Luke could not make out.

Kassor pivoted to squarely face Luke and called out in a rough voice, "Are you the man who shot at me in La Fonda?"

Luke did not like the threatening tone of the man's voice. Colonel Munroe's comment came to him, that he should have killed Kassor for it was dangerous to leave an enemy alive behind you, especially one who would knife a man in the back, and Kassor had been ready to stab Charlie Bell. Now Luke had a chance to correct his error. He checked the men for weapons and saw each was armed with a pistol in a holster on his side.

"Did somebody shoot at you, Kassor?" Luke said in a mocking tone. He continued his unhurried steps toward the two men blocking the sidewalk.

"If I knew for sure you were the one, I'd have something to say to you."

"Well it was me, so have your say," Luke replied in a taunting voice, and wanting to push the man into starting a fight. Watching Kassor, he spoke to the man with him, "Are you with Kassor in this?"

The man's eyes locked on Luke with a hard intensity. "Kassor can stand on his own," he said.

"Best that way." Luke continued to hold the man's eyes. "Once things start happening, a person could get hurt."

The man said nothing.

Luke halted and focused on the two men, everything else on the street fading away to nothing. He marked the positions of their hands, the tenseness of their bodies, their expressions. By the smooth, easy way the thin man moved, the steadiness of his eyes, the overall sureness of him, Luke judged he had been in gunfights before, and he had survived. Further, he could be the quicker of the two.

"What's your name?" Kassor asked.

"Coldiron," Luke said in a challenging voice.

"Why all this damn talking about his name?" said the thin man sharply. "If he took a shot at me, I'd sure as hell would do something about it."

"Just wanted to know the name of the man."

Luke sensed a growing reluctance in Kassor to continue the fight. He needed more prodding to make him fight.

"Get off the sidewalk Kassor and let a man through," Luke said in a harsh and mocking voice. "I've got a pretty woman waiting for me."

Kassor seemed to flinch at Luke's harsh words. Watching Luke, Kassor spoke to the second man. "Cleland wouldn't like it if I caused trouble in Santa Fe. Best I let it go this time."

The second man laughed. "Goddamn you, Kassor, for a coward."

Kassor jerked at the insult. Then he stiffened, staring across the space separating him from Luke. He grabbed for his pistol.

Luke drew, his hand catching the butt of his pistol, pulling it free of the holster, aiming, firing. The bullet broke Kassor's sternum bone, plowed through the lungs, and shattered his spine. The man was driven backward a step by the punch of the bullet. He seemed to trip and he fell onto the wooden sidewalk. Luke instantly swung his pistol the short arc to point at the second man.

The man raised his hands. "It was Kassor's fight, not mine," said the man with a sly smile.

Luke studied the man who had goaded Kassor into fighting Luke. A damn poor friend. No, not a friend, a trickster.

Luke regretted the killing. Still he couldn't let Kassor escape, for he was a coward who would kill a man from behind and that made him the most dangerous kind of enemy.

Now there was something that must be done. He turned to half a dozen men, who sensing a fight, had gathered in the street to watch. He recognized O'Fallon the saddle maker and called out to him. "O'Fallon did you see what happened?"

"Yes."

"Was it a fair fight?"

"Hell no. He didn't have a chance against you."

"That's not what I meant. Did he start the fight by threatening me?"

"That part's true."

"You be sure that you remember it that way if the military ask you."

F.M. Parker

Luke turned about and walked back the way he had come. Colonel Munroe must be made aware of Kassor's death. Luke knew the colonel would make an enquiry about the death of the man. However, since it was Kassor, and there were witnesses, nothing would come of it except a short written file describing the event.

Luke recalled Kassor mentioning the name Cleland. That was an odd coincidence, hearing the name shortly after Munroe telling about Cleland buying Mexican land pennies on the dollar.

***

The cloak of night's darkness was falling upon Santa Fe as Luke passed San Miguel Mission, a small adobe church that had been built by missionaries of the Spanish Catholic Church in 1610. He noted the church, and thought of the devout men who had come to this distant land and built it. If he had been a religious man, he might have stopped and asked for forgiveness for the killing. He continued on past the church in the direction of Liza's home.

A worry rode heavily upon Luke's shoulders as he drew close to the small adobe house where Liza lived. He had killed a man and now a short time later was going to see this lovely, gentle woman. What would she think if she knew what he had done? Would she even allow him to talk with her? Yet he could not pass up this evening without being with her.

Luke arrived at Liza's home and knocked on the door. It opened almost immediately and Liza stood smiling that lovely welcoming smile that she always gave him. Never had Luke seen a more beautiful smile than Liza's, the whole face, lips, cheeks and brown eyes all joining in. She did not realize the great value that welcoming smile held for Luke. During the nights, he would often lay and replay it across his inner eye and marvel at its beauty.

She reached out and caught him by the hand and drew him inside. Instantly the door closed, she was in his arms, pressing tightly against him.

"Oh, Luke, it's so good to see you. It has been much too long since you were here."

She tilted her face up to him and he kissed her, holding her yielding woman's body close against him. At last she drew back gave him a roguish look. His blood rushed fast and hot. He knew that look, that particular look that told him there would be pleasure given in the night. God! It was grand to make love to a woman who wanted to be loved.

Chapter Fifteen

Ernesto came awake in the early morning with Charlie shaking him by the shoulder. The face of his tall friend held a worried expression.

"What's wrong?" Ernesto asked.

"Come with me," Charlie replied. "We've got to talk. Don't wake Perla."

Ernesto pulled on his clothes and silently followed Charlie from the house. To his surprise, Charlie continued on across the rear yard and then through the small sheep pasture to the rim of the gorge of the Rio Grande. He did not stop there and began the descent of the rocky trail that clung to the steep side of the two hundred foot deep gorge. Ernesto followed without comment, watching his step with the injured leg.

Charlie reached the bottom of the gorge and halted in the pasture, a hundred feet wide strip of grass covered meadow that stretched ribbon-like along the river for nearly a quarter mile. He squatted on his haunches and broodingly regarded the eighteen colts he had stolen from Coldiron. One for each year of his age. The colts had stopped grazing and stood motionless with their feet tied to their shadows and their large brown eyes fastened upon the two men.

Ernesto seated himself on a large slab of lava that lay in the pasture. The piece of lava was part of the thick lava flow through which the Rio Grande had, over millions of years, carved its channel and now flowed at the bottom of the deep gorge. He waited for Charlie to tell what was on his mind.

Charlie felt the heavy weight of having stolen Coldiron colts. He recalled the time when he had decided to be a thief. That day had been in the late spring when Coldiron had brought forty horses to Santa Fe for sale by auction.

The event had not been held at the stock yards like other livestock sales, but on the main plaza of the town. It had been advertised in the local paper and had been the cause for a festive time with people coming to Santa Fe from miles around to attend. Many people wore their best clothing. Young Mexican men and women from the outlying ranchos came dressed in brightly colored riding clothing and mounted upon their own fine horses.

The men, women and children ringed the plaza, creating an open area in the center. As they waited for the auction to begin, the adults talked and the children romped and played. Charlie had laid aside his work at the blacksmith shop and came to stand among the throng.

Then Coldiron began to lead his horses one by one into the center of the plaza for the buyers to bid against each other for the animal. Coldiron horses were much in demand and the bidding had been fast with each bid jumping quickly over the one before.

That day, as the bidding for the last beautiful horse ended, Charlie, with about a hundred dollars in his pocket, decided to become a horse rancher. The only way he could achieve that goal was to become a thief and steal several filly colts. And then let nature take its course and make his heard grow. He wished the thought of stealing had not been planted in his mind by Ernesto's uncle. Ernesto had finally told Charlie the true relationship of the man.

"Ernesto, Luke Coldiron saved my life," Charlie said and turning to his friend.

"You told me."

"A man shouldn't steal from someone who has done that," Charlie said in a solemn tone. "So I'm going to return the colts to him."

"What!" Ernesto was shocked. He had been expecting something entirely different like Charlie telling him of his and Perla's relationship. He had been aware of it for the past several weeks. But not this, not returning the colts.

Ernesto spoke, tightly controlling his voice so as not to show his strong disapproval of Charlie's words, "How do you plan to do that?"

"I haven't figured that out yet."

"Why not just tell Coldiron we have them here and that he can come and get them? And then, of course, he'll hang us for stealing them."

Charlie's eyes fastened upon Ernesto's. He sensed the strong emotion Ernesto was holding within himself.

Ernesto continued to speak. "Charlie, how much money do you have?"

"A little over two hundred dollars."

"I have about the same amount. And that's after months of saving as much as we could. We might, and I say might, be able to buy two of these colts. So if we give the colts back, how do we start our rancho?"

"We can't. But it's the right thing to do. They're not spoils of war, something we want and just take. We're not at war with Coldiron."

"Well consider this. You only have to worry about giving back nine colts. That will be an easier job than giving back all eighteen."

Charlie gave Ernesto a quick, surprised look. "What do you mean?"

"The minute that I laid my hands on the colts and hid them down here on my pasture, I was as much a thief as you. That made me as likely as you to be hung for stealing them. Further that made me half owner of the colts. I sure don't plan to give my share back to Coldiron. I don't owe him anything."

"What?" The thought that Ernesto would not go along with returning the colts to Coldiron had never entered his thoughts. Yet Ernesto was correct, he was as much a thief as Charlie and did own half of the colts.

Ernesto spoke before Charlie could organize a reply. "Charlie, I understand how you feel. You could continue to be a blacksmith and I could go on farming this little piece of ground that barely provides Perla and me with a living. I want a horse rancho. I say we go on as we planned, take these colts to the Plains of San Augustin and build one. Kill as many of the bandits as we have to but build us a rancho."

Charlie turned to look at the colts that had drawn closer as the men had talked. He could not give back just half of the colts. How could he explain that to Coldiron, for he had meant to tell the man about taking them. Further, he had dreamed same as Ernesto that together they would build a grand rancho. He still wanted a rancho, he truly did.

Charlie faced Ernesto and locked eyes with him. "You're right, we can't give them back. We'll take them south to the Plains of San Augustin just as we planned."

"Now that's the way to think. If in four or five years after we have a herd of horses of our own, then you can give Coldiron back his colts."

"That's a long time in the future," Charlie replied, knowing the chance of that every happening was small. He fell silent and considering what the direction of their actions meant. One thing for certain, he had wronged a man who had saved his life.

"I say we go now. This very night." Ernesto did not want to give Charlie time to reconsider.

"All right," Charlie said. His face was glum with his thoughts.

"We must not be seen so it'd be best if we traveled cross country," Ernesto said. "There's a full moon so we'll travel only at night for the first couple of days."

"The colts can't travel far each day."

"We'll stop when they get tired," Ernesto said.

"You know this country, so what's the best way to go."

"I say we go west around the south end of the Jemez Mountains, cross the Rio Jemez and then turn south. I know most of that country. The year before I joined the army, my farther and I spent the summer there helping his cousin and his sons catch wild horses. One time we were far enough south that we camped at the base of Mesa Prieta. There was good spring water there. From the mesa we'll be able to see the Gallinas Mountains off at a far distance."

"Then what?"

"Then we just go on south past the Gallinas and there should be the Plains of San Augustin. Altogether, it should take us five to six days."

"I hope we're not seen by anybody."

"We may see a few Indians for there are some Zia and Navajo pueblos."

"Are they friendly?"

"We never had any trouble with them. They keep off by themselves. Our trouble will be with the bandits".

"Yeah, how to kill some and still be alive," Charlie said with a wry grin.

"And not get hung for stealing these colts," Ernesto added.

***

Daylight fled the deep gorge of the Rio Grande and night came stalking and filled it to the brim with darkness. In the east, the full-faced moon fought free of the layer of clouds lying on the horizon and threw its silver rays down upon the surface of the rippling water of the river.

In the bottom of the gorge, Charlie and Ernesto mounted their horses. The action of beginning the journey to the Plains of San Augustin was pulling Charlie's thoughts away from his doubts about keeping Coldiron's colts. He was glad for the reprieve.

All was ready for the journey. He had ridden to Santa Fe to get his bedroll, and to buy a supply of food, gunpowder and balls for their pistols and carbines, and sufficient rope for staking out the animals to graze. Ernesto had left most of his money for Perla and a note telling her that he and Charlie had taken jobs to guard a wagon train to Mexico City and would be gone for several weeks. That she should tend the farm until they returned.

Charlie and Ernesto, each towing behind them nine colts tied nose to tail with short ropes, waded into the swift current of the Rio Grande. The water parted for the strong legs of the animals. It gradually deepened and the animals sank to their bellies, and then deeper still and the colts were forced to swim. Only their heads showed above the surface. Several feet further along, the churning hooves of the scared colts found the stony bottom of the river and the colts, all wet and glistening in the moonlight, rose up from the water. The men and animals left the water and climbed the far bank. The river healed it self behind them and retained no evidence of their passing.

The two riders with their stolen animals hurried to the west into the moon lit pinion pine and juniper forest shrouding the flanks of Jemez Mountains looming thousands of feet above them on the right.

Chapter Sixteen

The two young Ute brothers, Thunder Hawk and Jumping Eagle rode into Santa Fe mounted upon two of Luke Coldiron's horses that they had acquired as part of their wages as horse wranglers. Each man led a horse that he had trained for Luke to deliver to Armendaris.

The two men were dressed in dark gray trousers and flannel shirts, Thunder's shirt of a blue color and Eagle's red. Both wore gray hats the color of their trousers. There were no spurs on their boots for they had trained their mounts so well that the rider's voice, or a touch of the reins on their necks, or the feel of a boot heel was all that was needed to get the desired action from their steeds.

"Take off your gun," Thunder Hawk said as they rode along the street. He was the older by two years.

"I don't like being in this town without wearing my gun," Jumping Eagle said in a sour tone.

"Luke said we must always put our guns out of sight when we're here."

Each man unbuckled his gun belt with holstered pistol and stored it in his saddlebags.

"I've got a feeling there will be trouble today," Jumping Eagle said, and watching warily around at the people coming and going along the street.

"If that happens, then we'll take out our guns and shoot somebody."

"I'd like to do that."

"We'll look for Luke at the La Fonda first," Thunder Hawk said.

"That's where we'll most likely find him," Jumping Eagle agreed.

They rode on along the street, drawing the eyes of the men, women and children who were out and about in the town. A larger boy recognized the Wolf Trap brand and shouted out, "Horse Killer will hang you Indians for stealing his horses."

The brothers rode on, giving no sign that they heard the boy's words, and entered the plaza. At La Fonda, they dismounted and fastened their mounts to the tie post in front of the establishment.

"Wait here while I check inside for Luke," Thunder Hawk said. He entered La Fonda.

Jumping Eagle stepped upon the sidewalk and leaned against the wall near the entrance and turned to watch the street.

A couple of minutes later, Thunder Hawk emerged from La Fonda. "Luke isn't here. And nobody knows where he is."

"Let's ask his woman," said Jumping Eagle. "Maybe she knows where he might be."

"She surely is a beautiful woman."

Jumping Eagle smiled at the words. "Enough for two women."

"That she does."

They mounted and rode from the plaza and along San Francisco Street. They halted in front of Liza Donnelly's shop.

"I'll go inside and ask about Luke," Thunder Hawk said as he swung down from his horse.

"I'll go with you," said Jumping Eagle as he too dismounted.

"I don't need your help."

"I want to see her too."

The young men grinned at each other with understanding. They stepped upon the sidewalk and entered Liza's shop.

Liza looked up from the sewing machine where she was stitching the hem of a dress. She recognized Thunder Hawk and Jumping Eagle from having seen them with Luke. They were swiftly removing their hats in respect to her.

Hello," she said and gave them a friendly smile. She rose from the sewing machine and came part way across the room toward the two young men.

With their eyes locked on Liza, Thunder Hawk and Jumping Eagle bobbed their heads in acknowledgement of her greeting.

"What can I do for you?" Liza said. She saw that expression in their eyes that she often noted in the eyes of men she met. That look often angered her, but in the eyes of these two young men, she accepted it with a feeling of amused pleasure.

"We're looking for Luke, Mrs. Donnelly," said Thunder Hawk. "Do you know where we might find him?"

"He told me that he had a meeting with Colonel Munroe and several other ranchers at the Governor's Palace. You could look there."

The two men did not move, continuing to hold their eyes upon Liza. Then Thunder Hawk jerked with the realization that he was staring. He jabbed Jumping Eagle in the ribs. "Let's have a look at the Governor's Palace."

"Right," said Jumping Eagle and flinching at the jab in the ribs.

They pivoted about and hastened from the shop.

Liza laughed softly to herself as she noted the two brothers were clothed in garments very similar to those Luke wore, except for the brightly colored shirts.

***

"There's Luke." Jumping Eagle said to Thunder Hawk, pointing ahead at the group of men coming from the Governor's Palace, a long, brown colored adobe building, on the east side of the plaza.

"I see him."

Luke, seeing Jumping Eagle and Thunder Hawk, separated from the other ranchers and came to meet his two wranglers. They were late and that wasn't like them. That could mean trouble.

"I know that we're late," Thunder Hawk said quickly, "Something came up that we had to take care of."

"Something damn important," Jumping Eagle added.

Luke nodded at the quick words of explanation from the two brothers. He liked the pair. They were very amiable, hard-working and dependable.

"Well climb down off your horses and tell me about it."

"Could we eat while we talk?" Thunder Hawk said. "We haven't had a bite since daylight."

"Sure. Ride down to La Fonda and I'll buy you a steak."

The two brothers reined their horse away, and leading the two extra horses intended for Armendaris, rode off along the street. Luke walked along beside them.

***

In the dining area of La Fonda and while three large steaks were being fried, Luke said. "Now tell me what was so important that it made you late."

Thunder Hawk spoke. "Well, we were on our way here yesterday morning when we saw a group of mares watering at the creek. They were the ones that graze on the mountain on the southwest side of the rancho. Some of them had no colts."

"And most of them had full udders which showed that they had had colts by their side until recently." Jumping Eagle said.

Thunder hawk nodded in agreement. "The udder of one of them was leaking milk which meant that she had a colt nursing until the past two or three days. Well, we had to find out what had happened to the missing colts. So we rode up on the mountain looking for lion or wolf kills. We found where a lion had killed an elk calf and where a wolf had killed a young deer. But nothing else."

"We saw something odd," Jumping Eagle said. "The colts with the mares were mostly little studs. It was the fillies that were missing."

"Damnation," exclaimed Luke. "Someone is stealing the colts to start a herd of their own. How many are missing?"

"We'd guess at least fifteen, could be more," Thunder Hawk replied. "Once we knew that they had been stolen, we began to look for tracks. Couldn't find any. Then we found this hanging on a stone fence that closed a gap in the rimrock." He pulled a hand-size piece of burlap from his pants pocket and handed it to Luke.

"So they had their feet wrapped in burlap," Luke said. "Careful son-of-bitches."

"Just one man and one colt," Thunder Hawk said. "And he had the colt's feet wrapped too. Once we knew about the burlap and what to look for, we tracked him and the colt for about two miles."

"But we lost him when he crossed a lava flow," Jumping Eagle said quickly with explanation. He regretted having failed to follow the thief to where he had hidden the colt.

"Which way was he headed?"

"Toward Santa Fe," Thunder Hawk said.

Luke silently considered the information. The thief would have to pay. Pay very dearly.

The steaks came and the three of them began to eat. The brothers fell too at the steaks with knives and forks. They waited for Luke to speak first.

Luke finished his steak and shoved his plate away. "One man stealing one colt at a time," he said, breaking the silence. "That means a cautious man, and one who has a place to hide the colts until they can be branded and then heal. Where is that place most likely to be?" He paused and then continued to speak, answering his own question. "It would be in the canyon of the Rio Grande or a spring in the mountains far away from other people. My first choice would be the canyon."

The brothers nodded in unison.

"Few people ever go down in the canyon," Jumping Eagle said.

"And there are no lions in the canyon," Thunder Hawk added. "They're all in the mountains."

"There's something else about the thief," Jumping Eagle said. "He's a tall fellow. We measured his steps."

"A tall man who steals one colt at a time." Luke rubbed his chin. "He'll be taller when we get done hanging him."

"When do we start looking for him?" asked Jumping Eagle.

"For now, go back to the ranch and bring all the horses into headquarters and brand the colts."

"That'll give the fellow more time to hide the colts," Jumping Eagle said.

"They're already hidden. Don't say anything about them. I'll take the two horses you've brought and deliver them as promised to Pedro Armendaris. That'll take me a week. When I get back, we'll find the thieves and hang him."

Chapter Seventeen

Charlie and Ernesto pulled their horse to a halt and sat in their saddles and stared at the billowing, swirling dust storm roll menacingly down upon them from the northwest. The weary colts stopped and stood quietly behind them.

"We're in for a bad one," Ernesto said.

"Yeah."

The dust storm was a tan colored monster rising to fill a quarter of the sky. It stretched for miles left and right, its northern portion sweeping across the playa on their right and its southern portion pounding the hills on their left. Already the storm's frontal winds were striking the two riders and their mounts, flopping the brims of the men's hats and making streaming flags of the horses' tails.

This was the middle of the afternoon of the fifth day after leaving Ernesto's farm on the Rio Grande. They had avoided being seen except for three Zia Indian horsemen they had encountered along the Rio Puerco. The Indians had not ridden close enough as they passed to make out much about Charlie and Ernesto and the colts.

Their present course was taking them along the edge of a playa some half dozen miles across. Surrounding the playa on all side were dome shaped hills covered with grass and studded with low growing juniper and patches of bushes. The playa was a depressed area into which streams from the surrounding hills emptied their spring time flow of water; having no outlet through which the water could escape, it collected there to form a shallow lake. During the summer and autumn of the year, the water was sucked away by the sun to leave behind an ever shrinking body of water, until nothing remained but mud, and then that sometimes dried to leave a barren land behind.

"The colts will be scared by the storm and will hurt themselves if we leave them tied in a string," said Charlie.

"Best we tie them singly to some of those junipers."

Charlie and Ernèsto dismounted and hurriedly tied each colt securely with its lead rope to the trunk of a sturdy juniper. They tied their mounts in the same manner.

"That rock will give us some shelter from the storm," Charlie said, pointing to a close by large gray boulder as tall as their shoulders.

They hastened to the boulder, sat down on the lee side, pulled their hats down tightly on their heads and tied their bandanas over their mouths and noses.

The winds increased in strength, picking up the dry silt and fine sand of the playa to send it streaming in hundreds of ground currents. The wind rapidly increased to a gale as the front of the sandstorm charged ever closer. It leapt the last quarter mile with amazing speed, and with the wind shrieking a wild song, the blizzard of choking dust fell upon the men and stung their faces like fire. The dust searched for their eyes and the men squeezed them shut. They humped their shoulders and endured the pounding.

The horses and colts squealed with fear, stomped the ground and strained to tear loose from their tie ropes. Unable to break free and flee, they turned their rumps to the cutting, blinding dust.

Overhead the sun burned scarlet though the dust.

***

Somewhat more than an hour after the sandstorm struck Charlie and Ernesto, it ended its slashing onslaught upon them and blew itself away to the southeast. The men climbed to their feet, slapped the dust off their clothing as best they could and breathed in the clean air.

They hawked and spat on the ground, uncorked their canteens and drank water to wash the dust from their throats.

Charlie shook his nearly empty canteen. "We need to find water."

"I don't like dry camps, so let's get traveling."

They tied the colts in a string, nine of them nose to tail for each man and rode off along the edge of the playa.

Charlie looked out across the brush-covered hills. There was no sign man had ever passed this way. Yet he knew the Indians had been here for countless generations. He turned to survey the broad playa. Nothing moved upon that naked, desolate land. Wait! Wait! Something did move far away at the limit of his vision, a small black object that rose and fell, to rise and fall again, and then again. The waves of heated air distorted the image and made it impossible to identify.

"What do you think that black thing that's moving out there could be?" Charlie asked and pointed off across the playa.

Ernesto shaded his eyes from the slanting rays of the sun and stared. "It's way off and so must have some size to it. It could be a man that's hurt. But I don't know why in hell he would be out there in that godforsaken place. We've seen antelope, deer and wild horses, so it could be

F.M. Parker

one of them that got spooked by the storm and ran out there and got stuck in some mud."

"I say we go and take a look in case it's a man and needs help."

They reined their mounts to the side and rode out on- to the playa. Minutes later, in the deepest portion of the playa, they came to a wide area of mud with a small pool of water of half an acre or so in its center. Between them and the water, an animal buried to its chest in the mud, struggled fiercely to break free of its entrapment, its head jerking and its mud caked mouth sucking at the air. The animal had tried to reach water and had found what could be death.

Charlie called out. "It's a horse."

"I'd say a yearling."

As Charlie and Ernesto drew closer, the horse con- tinued to struggle frantically to tear free. Then it abruptly ceased moving and, and with its brown eyes huge with fear, stared at the men.

"It'll die if we don't get it free," Ernesto said.

"Let's see if we can pull it loose."

"I'm lighter weight than you," Ernesto said. "I'll wade out there and tie a rope around it."

He dismounted and leaned against his mount while pulling off his boots. "I don't want to lose them in the mud," he said and grinned at Charlie.

Ernesto waded barefooted into the mud with his lariat. With each step, the mud was ever gooier, and he sank ever deeper, until he was laboring mightily to pull each leg free to take another step.

"No wonder it got stuck," he called to Charlie.

Ernesto struggled onward and finally reached the horse. He crawled upon its back and leaned down and worked the rope around its chest just behind its front legs. Finally succeeding with the placement of the rope, he fought his way back to dry land.

While Ernesto scraped mud from his legs and feet, Charlie fastened the end of the rope around the horn of his saddle.

"We'd both best help the horse pull."

"Give me a minute to get my boots on."

With the horse backing away and the rope taught and the men adding their strength and pulling with all of their strength, the mired horse came free of the mud and was dragged upon dry ground. The rescued animal lay motionless and breathing heavily, watching the men as it had done throughout the operation. After a minute or so it struggled to its feet and stood with its legs splayed and trembling with weakness. The men began to rake the mud off the rescued yearling and sling it away.

Ernesto backed away a few steps and eyed the Yearling. "He's a mud cake, but even so he looks like a good horse. We should take him with us."

"At least until we get the mud off and can see what he looks like. You know about wild horses, so tell me why this one would be out here all alone? Where's the rest of the herd?"

"He was born back in the spring last year. That makes him a year and a half old. At that age they start noticing the mares and starting sniffing around them. Well, the herd stallion doesn't like that and so he drives the young studs away from the herd. Sometimes they form groups for company. We call them bachelor studs. This one just happened to be alone."

The yearling started to move away from the men and Ernesto hastened to it and placed the lariat around its neck. "You're going to stays with us."

He turned to Charlie. "If we take it slow, I think this fellow can make it to water."

"Let's getting moving," Charlie said. He had a strong feeling that Coldiron had discovered some of his colts were missing. The farther south Ernesto and Charlie went, the greater was their safety from being hung.

Leading the yearling on the lariat, and the colts on their tethers, Charlie and Ernesto rode onward to the south and left the playa behind.

***

"That's the Gallinas Mountains," Ernesto said and pointed south past the flank of Mesa Prieta.

Charlie stared through the deepening dusk of the day at the mountains on the distant horizon. "How far away do you judge they are?"

"I say it'll take us about a day to reach them."

Only a minute before, Charlie and Ernesto had reached the spring at the base of Mesa Prieta that Ernesto had camped at with his father, uncle and cousins those days past while capturing wild horses. The mesa was a massive mound of rock towering above them three hundred feet and stretching north and south some eight miles. The spring, flowing several gallons of water a minute, came clear and sparkling from the top of an impervious layer of rock. Below the spring and irrigated by its water, was a meadow of an acre or so. Elsewhere around, aged junipers were scattered about.

For the past half mile or so as the two men approached the green area of meadow that told of the presence of the spring, they had scrutinized the land closely. Finding it deserted and safe they had approached. Now they lay down and drank where the water came pure from the rock heart of the mesa.

Charlie raised his head from the water and took a long breath. "Damn good water."

He rose to his feet and wiped the water from his mouth with the back of his hand. He swung his view to look about at this new land. He stiffened. "Wolf," he called out and pointed.

Beneath the outstretched limbs of an old gnarled juniper some hundred feet distant, a large male wolf of a deep gray, almost black color, stood motionless. Its keen eyes were staring unblinkingly at the men. Its muzzle was lifted and its nostrils were expanded as it pulled slow deep breaths of the air and testing the men's scent. The wolf showed intense curiosity of the men.

Charlie watched the animal with fascination. He knew the animal was taking in everything visible, everything heard, smelled, and things that could only be sensed in that wolf brain. He felt no alarm at the wolf, only a great curiosity.

"Well, I'll be damned," Ernesto said. "It's been there all this time and watching us." As Ernesto spoke, the wolf turned and loped effortlessly away, seeming to glide, to float over the ground.

In the thickening shadows of falling night, the men went to the horses and colts and staked them out tethered to picket ropes on the meadow to graze the wild green grass. They brought the yearling up close to the spring, and splashing water upon it, began to wash it free of the dry caked mud that covered it. As more and more of the yearling became visible, Ernesto commented again and again upon its find features, the length of its legs, the depth of its chest, and its alert watchful eyes showing its intelligence.

As the yearling shook itself to fling off the last of the water, Ernesto backed away from it and grabbed Charlie by the shoulder. "Madre de Dios, he is beautiful."

"He's a fine animal that's for sure." Charlie smiled broadly at the discovery.

"He's one of those rare throwbacks to the original Spanish Barbs," Ernesto said. "The horses that were brought to Mexico by the Conquistadores."

"I've read that our wild horses came from some of those horses that got loose."

"Let's make him our stud," said Ernesto. "He's a yearling. In two more years he will be three and old enough to make love with our beautiful fillies, who will be just the right age for breeding."

"He's black, the very color we should have for the stud of these dark colored fillies," Charlie chuckled. "Now we have the horses we need to build us a great rancho."

"I told you we should keep the fillies," Ernesto said.

"Coldiron could still catch and hang us."

"Maybe. And maybe not. Our luck has been good."

'Lucky streaks always end."

***

The last of the daylight burned down to black ash and night fell upon the land. In the darkness, Charlie and Ernesto spread their bedrolls on the meadow grass near the spring, placed their carbines and pistols close to hand, and lay wearily down. To hide their presence, they made no fire. The evening meal had been made of cheese and crackers and dried fruit and more cold fresh water.

Charlie lay on his back and rested, listening to the murmur of the spring as it tumbled gently over its pebbly bottom. He watched the round yellow moon break free of the eastern rim of the earth and begin its silent climb up its ancient, sky path across the high, night heavens. Beside him, he heard Ernesto stirring as he made himself comfortable on his blanket.

Ernesto spoke, "Charlie, we were lucky to find the yearling. I believe he will give us great colts."

"We're two lucky thieves," Charlie said in a gloomy tone.

"I know you feel bad about stealing Coldiron's colts. But I don't. Look at it this way. We're just little thieves stealing from a bigger thief."

"A bigger thief? I've never heard that Coldiron ever stole anything." Charlie rose up on an elbow and looked at Ernesto's night shrouded from.

"Oh, yeah. Well he's a thief all right. That big valley that he claims as his rancho is stolen. And the horses that he chose to breed his famous horses were also stolen."

"How do you figure that?" Charlie said, astounded by Ernesto's words.

"That valley and the horses that grazed there belonged to the Ute Indians for hundreds, even thousands of years. Coldiron went there with his rifle and pistol and took the land from them. He killed some of their warriors when they tried to run him away. Charlie, he's a thief and killer. So I don't feel guilty about taking the colts. If he catches up with us and tries to take the colts back, I'll shoot him quick as I can. I'm sure not letting him hang me. Or you."

Charlie fell silent, pondering Ernesto's words. Then he spoke. "I'm betting that Coldiron doesn't see what he's done as stealing."

"Most likely he doesn't for white men don't think Indians have ownership of land. But how he feels doesn't change the fact that he stole the Ute's land and horses."

The truth of what Ernesto said came full blown to Charlie. His white man's eyes had been blind until this moment as to what Coldiron had done. Further he knew why Ernesto had seen the truth. The same thing had happened to his people. The Americans with their rifles and cannon had invaded Mexican land, killed thousands of the Mexican warriors and claimed for themselves half of the land of that proud nation.

"You're awfully quiet," Ernesto said. "Do you disagree with what I said?"

"No. I understand and see that you're correct. But have you considered that by your reasoning, Mexicans are also thieves. They too have stolen land from the Indians and killed hundreds, maybe thousands of them when they resisted?"

"Damnation. That was so long ago that I had forgotten that the Indians were here before my people came and built their towns and ranchos. But, yes, we're thieves too."

"There's nothing that will change any of this," Charlie said. "The Indians will never get their land back." He lay down and again watched the moon in its silent climb up the sky.

"And I don't think Mexicans will ever get their land back," Ernesto said in a sad voice.

Spoils of war, thought Charlie.

"Does it make you feel any better to know Coldiron is a thief?" Ernesto said. "A bigger thief than us?"

"Maybe a little. Seems like everybody is a thief."

Ernesto's voice came hard out of the darkness. "Charlie, Coldiron may find us. I know you feel that you owe him for saving your life. But I owe him nothing and I'm not going to let him hang me. Or hang you. I'll kill him first."

Charlie did not want to fight Coldiron. The man had saved his life and he owed him for that. Even if Coldiron was a thief and murderer.

***

Charlie awoke in the night to an explosion of barks, yaps, and howls rising shrill and penetrating not a half mile away south along the base of the mesa.

Ernesto spoke from the darkness. "That's wolves rounding up their pack for the night's hunt. Sounds like there're about five or six of them."

"They're sure making a racket."

"They're hungry," Ernesto said. "They don't much bother full grown horses, but the fillies could tempt them."

"And that big fellow we saw knows about them too."

Charlie lay and listened to the strident cries of the wolves rushing unbound across the land. As he listened to their voices, the barks and yaps and howls combined into a harmonious melding of pitch and tone and volume that resembled a human yodeling, a surprisingly pure sound that was truly pleasant. He cupped his ears in his hands and turned in the direction of the song. As he eavesdropped upon the wolves, he sensed the kinship each member of the pack must have for all the others, and their readiness for the hunt.

After but a few seconds, the joining of animal voices broke apart and once again they were but a clamoring of barks and yaps and howls of the wolf pack. The volume lessened and then the last yap sounded and silence fell.

Charlie pictured the wolves, so sure of themselves in the darkness with their night-seeing eyes and ready for the chase and the kill, loping off over the land led by their leader, a large, strong animal. Perhaps the very one they had seen. He was growing to like this land of New Mexico very much.

He was still thirsty after the long warm day. He rose from his blanket and went to the spring and knelt and leaned to look into the flat pool of water glistening in the moonlight. A face rose up out of the water and stared at him. He jerked back at the abrupt appearance. Then he chuckled in rebuke to himself for his reaction to the face. It was his own.

"Hello, Charlie Bell, you horse thief," he whispered, very low so that Ernesto could not hear him and think him crazy.

He leaned down to the water and drank along with the reflection. Satisfied, he returned to his blanket and lay watching the golden sphere of the moon climb the starry sky. How gentle the moment felt when the day had ended without trouble, and further, they had found water, and now Ernesto slept and the colts and horses rested.

He was still awake when the star-filled sky, whirling about its axis, swept the Seven Sisters of the Pleiades right up overhead. Finally he drifted into sleep with his ears cocked toward the colts, hoping the wolves did not come.

Chapter Eighteen

The dust, lying thick on El Camino Real, the main street of Socorro, splashed up like thick, brown water from under the iron-shod hooves of Luke's mare and the two horses he led. A cloud of the dust hung on the air and trailed along behind, marking his path as he made his way along. Luke was riding south to deliver the two horses to Armendaris as promised.

Luke knew the town for he had passed through it a few times in the past and had spent a couple of nights in the local hotel. The town, its population almost entirely Mexican, stretched along the El Camino Real for nearly a mile. The Rio Grande flowed in its channel to the west a quarter mile. Between the town and the river were gardens and orchards irrigated with water from the river. He could see men, women and children gathering the late ripening pears and apples. Some of the men were standing on ladders to reach the higher fruit.

One big pear tree held a boy of eight or nine high up in its branches and pulling pears and tossing them down to a man with a basket on the ground. The boy climbed to the topmost branch, pulled the last pear and tossed it down. Holding onto a branch with one hand and waving the other high above his head, he shouted out loudly to proclaim his bravery with his climb. Luke laughed silently.

Anxious to return and begin the hunt for the thieves who had stolen his colts, Luke had traveled swiftly from Santa Fe the past three days. During the journey when the mount he rode showed weariness from carrying his weight, he had moved his saddle to another horse, and then when that animal grew tried, to another. With this change of mounts, he had traveled the miles speedily. He was weary from the hard riding.

The day was ending and Luke decided he would stop in Socorro for the night. He would have a cool bath, a good meal and sleep in a soft bed and not a blanket on the ground. In the morning, he would continue on the last distance to the Armendaris rancho.

He rode onward toward a restaurant and the hotel adjacent to it. As he drew close, he saw a tall, rail thin man sitting on a chair on the porch of the hotel. It was the man, the trickster, who had been with Kassor in Santa Fe. His hat was shoved back and his booted feet were propped up on a second chair. He wore a pistol. His relaxed attitude gave him the appearance of having been seated on the porch for a lengthy time. At the moment, his sight was fastened upon Luke and his horses.

As Luke drew his mare to a halt in front of the hotel, a pigeon dove down from the rooftop of the nearby restaurant where it had been perched and landed in the street. The bird, watching warily with its black eyes, began to peck at a scrap of bread that had been cast into the street from the restaurant.

Almost immediately, a large gray cat darted from under the porch of the restaurant. All teeth and claws, the cat launched itself at its prey. The alert pigeon saw the cat and leapt into flight, fleeing into the sky with a flutter of wings and fear.

The cat landed, its feet puffing the dust up in a yellow cloud where the bird had been an instant before. The cat was invisible for a moment. Then it came out of the dust, shook itself, and stalked all rigid and angry back in under the porch.

"Mister Cat missed his dinner that time," said the man sitting on the hotel porch.

"Looks like it," Luke replied.

"First time I've seen him miss," said the man.

Luke said nothing.

The man nodded at the two horses Luke led. "Good looking horses."

"They'll do until better ones come along," Luke said.

Luke dismounted and tied the mare and the other two horses in front of the hotel. As Luke passed the seated man, he noted the spurs strapped to the heels of his boots resting on the chair. The spurs had the largest rowels, something over an inch in diameter, he had ever seen. Each spike of the rowels was filed to a sharp point.

The man noted Luke's sight upon the spurs. "You like my spurs," he said, and his long slit of a mouth stretched wide as he grinned up at Luke. "The rowels are made of silver."

"No. Too hard on a horse."

"They sure enough make a horse move quick when you want it to," said the man. He began to chuckle as if enjoying the thought of spurring a horse.

At the man's chuckle and his challenging look, Luke felt the urge to strike him in the face. He controlled the urge with an effort. He turned away and entered the hotel and approached the desk.

"I need a room for tonight," he said in Spanish to the clerk behind the desk.

"I have one," replied the Mexican.

Luke turned and chucked a thumb at the man on the hotel porch. "How long has he been here?"

"This is the second day."

"What's his name?"

"He signed his name as Tucker. Ben Tucker."

"What's his business?"

"I don't know. He just sits there on the porch and watches the people come and go on the street."

"Did he talk with anybody?"

"Yes, to some senoritas that passed on the street. I didn't hear what he said to them. But they didn't like it."

"I can bet why," Luke said.

Luke paid for the room and left the hotel. He ignored the man on the porch and went to his horses. As he untied the animals, something caught his attention and he turned and looked. In the northwest, a tan colored mass of swirling dust stretching for miles both left and right was rolling down upon Socorro.

"Damnation," he muttered.

He quickly led the horses along the street a half block to a building with a sign identifying it as a livery stable. He spoke to the Mexican who answered his call at the door. "Give each horse a half gallon of grain and all the hay it will eat. And keep them inside."

"Yes, senor," replied the man. "I will take very good care of them." He smiled broadly when Luke paid with silver.

Luke hastened across the street and into the restaurant as the first dusty breath of the storm fell upon the town. He relaxed and breathed in the tantalizing aroma of freshly baked bread wafting to him. He would have a leisurely meal and wait out the storm in the restaurant.

He ordered a huge meal, choosing roast beef as the main course when the elderly Mexican woman came to his table and informed him that it was freshly made. Then he sat and waited with anticipation for the food and watched through the front window of the restaurant as the street filled with a fast flowing river of swirling dust.

Chapter Nineteen

In the long shadows of the day, Charlie and Ernesto halted their horses and sat their saddles and stared up at the round-topped, pine clad Gallinas Mountains towering above them. Behind them the weary colts hung their heads and rested.

"The Gallinas Mountains at last," Ernesto said. "Uncle Carlos said the Plains of San Augustin lies just beyond them."

"Instead of going around them, what do you say to us camping up there tonight?" Charlie said and pointing up at a protruding shoulder on the forested flank of the mountain. "The slope isn't too steep and from up there we can get a good look at the Plains first thing in the morning."

"And that could help us figure out where to start looking for the land for our rancho," Ernesto replied.

"Right," said Charlie. "And we'd better hurry if we're going to make it up there before dark," he added, looking at the sun barely a finger's width above the western horizon.

The two men touched their mounts with the heels of their boots and began the climb. The yearling and the colts trailed along wearily behind on their lead ropes.

***

Charlie and Ernesto traveled steadily up through the juniper and pine forest clothing the flank of the mountain. They reached the shoulder of the mountain just as the sun disappeared below the horizon. They hurriedly began a detour around a huge treacherous slope of fallen rock leaning against the mountain side and blocking their view to the south.

They broke clear of the rocks and a thousand feet below them lay the Plains of San Augustin, a broad expanse of grass-covered land extending as far as the eye could see to the south. The frail light, reflecting down from the heavens, colored the land a grayish purple. Mountains, miniaturized by a far distance, rimmed the Plains on the far away west side.

"Now that's a big piece of country," Charlie said, fascinated by the immense size of the Plains.

Ernesto pointed to the mountains lying several miles to the southeast. "That would be the Magdalena Mountains where Uncle Carlos has his rancho,"

"It'll take some long hard riding to find the best place for our rancho. And it'll be winter in a couple of months."

Charlie paused as a thought came to him. "Since your uncle knows this land, do you think he'd help us choose the best place for our rancho?"

"We'll ask him."

"Best we make camp quick before it gets dark."

Ernesto pointed off to the right around the mountain side. "I see some cottonwoods over there about a quarter mile. They like to have their roots in water. Might be some for us."

In the growing shadows of the coming night, Charlie and Ernesto reached the grove of cottonwoods and found a small stream winding its course down from the higher elevations of the mountain. They immediately led the horses and colts to the stream and the thirsty animals lowered their heads and began to drink.

As the animals drank, Charlie and Ernesto quenched their thirst just upstream from them. Then they drove stout wooden picket stakes into the ground along both sides of the stream where the grass grew. When the animals finished drinking, they tied each one to a stake by its picket rope. The hungry animals immediately began to graze.

"Your uncle said this was bandit country, so best we have just a small fire," Charlie said. "They'll find out soon enough that we're here and come to steal our colts."

"Let's build it there behind that boulder. That'll hide it from below." Ernesto pointed at the boulder lying in the edge of the cottonwoods.

As the animals grazed, the men made their camp, spreading their blankets upon the ground under the largest of the cottonwoods. They gather dry branches from a dead juniper and built a small fire. They ate food from their saddlebags, then rested wearily on their blankets and watched the flames devour the juniper wood.

Charlie noted a darkening of the night and looked upward. Thick clouds were moving in from the west and hiding the moon.

"I hope it doesn't rain tonight," he said.

Ernesto looked up at the clouds. "I'm glad we're here even if it pours rain."

Charlie said nothing, staring up at the sky now obscured by the clouds and very dark. The great bulk of the mountain looming close over them added to the blackness of the night. He felt danger close upon them.

He turned and looked at Ernesto resting on his blanket with his head propped up on his saddle. He enjoyed his small friend's companionship. More than that, he knew he could always depend upon Ernesto's courage should the danger he felt find them.

"Something bothering you?" Ernesto said, rising up on an elbow.

"Just thinking about the future."

"It's going to be a long, tough job to build our rancho."

Charlie said nothing.

At ease in each other's company, they lay silently on their blankets and listened to the crackling of the burning juniper wood and watched the flames.

As the men watched, a pale gray moth, the size of a silver dollar, fluttered out of the mountain darkness in that jerky style of flight with which their kind move and into the edge of the bubble of yellow light created by the fire. The tiny aviator stopped abruptly there as if evaluating the fire. With its little wings stroking the air to hold it airborne, it held its position as its little antenna waved about testing the air. Then abruptly the little flyer darted toward the fire. For an instant the moth was a beautiful glistening figure in the firelight. Then a finger of flame reached up and engulfed the moth and its body flashed one single spark as it was transformed into a bit of ash.

"I've never see a moth do that before," Charlie said in amazement.

"Neither have I," said Ernesto. "The heat always scares them away. I hope it wasn't a bad omen."

"I'd like to think it was just a crazy moth."

"A big mistake. Crazy or not."

The death, the cremation of the moth, brought a heavy sadness to lie on Charlie. To change his thoughts, he rose to his feet and went to check the colts. He walked among them, their black forms but darker pieces of the night. He slid his hands over their hairy backs as they ignored him and grazed the mountain grass. He was glad they had accepted him. He tested their picket ropes, pulling stoutly on them to be certain that they were soundly anchored in the ground. They must not wander off in the night. Satisfied with the animals' tethers, he turned and retraced his steps to the fire.

"Everything all right?" Ernesto said.

"Yes."

Charlie lay down with his feet to the fire. He pulled his blanket over him for the night had acquired a chill, a promise that the autumn was wearing thin and winter was growing ever closer. Or was it Coldiron drawing ever closer.

***

In the early hour of the brisk autumn morning, Luke rode at a trot south upon El Camino Real lying under a sky of endless sapphire blue. The horses, well rested, moved along smartly. The only sound to break the silence was the strike of the horses' iron shod hooves upon the stony roadway. The wind of the day before was gone, leaving not a whisper. High above, half a dozen vultures with their keen sense of smell, were tracing wide, swinging circles as they searched for the odor of something dead on the ground.

Luke was looking forward to meeting Pedro Armendaris, a man he had known for several years. He thought Armendaris would approve of the horses he was bringing him. Once that business was completed, Luke would hasten back to Santa Fe and begin the search for his stolen colts.

The sound of a galloping horse came to Luke and he turned to look behind. Tucker, the skinny man he had seen on the porch of the hotel the evening before was overtaking Luke. A warning blew through Luke's mind and he reined his horse so that he could face the man.

Tucker pulled his mount to a halt with a hard, tight rein and the hooves of the horse sliding to a stop on the hard ground. "Howdy, Coldiron," he called out in a friendly voice. "You're an early riser and I almost missed catching you."

"What's on your mind?" Luke said, feeling a strong disliking for the man.

"I've thought about your horses and want to buy one." Tucker pulled a leather pouch from a pocket and shook it to jingle the coins together. "I'll pay in gold and not paper. What do you want for one of the horses?"

"They're both sold."

"Damn, that's a shame. I sure do want one of them."

Luke shrugged and said nothing. He would not have sold the man a horse even if he had one for sale.

Tucker sat for a moment and stared at Luke. "Oh, hell. I've lost out before. So long." He reined his mount around and walked it back toward Socorro.

Luke turned to continue his journey south toward the Armendaris rancho. After a short moment, a disturbing thought came to him. Tucker had merely reined his horse away and left at a walk. At a walk! And a man who liked to use his spurs. Luke whirled to look behind.

Tucker, now nearly fifty yards distant, had pulled his rifle from its scabbard and was preparing to dismount. Luke instantly realized that Tucker had ridden out of accurate pistol range and was now preparing to shoot him with a rifle. But why?

At the moment, the reason was not important. Luke grabbed for his rifle in its scabbard under his right leg. Even as his hand closed on the weapon, he knew that he could never beat Tucker to the first shot. Further Tucker would be a deadly marksman with a rifle, otherwise he would not have chosen that weapon.

As Tucker pulled his right boot from the stirrup to step down upon the ground, the sharp rowel of the big silver spur raked his horse's ribs. The animal flinched and shied away from the painful stab of the spur. Tucker was thrown off balance and staggered two steps before he caught himself. He pivoted to face Luke, brought the rifle to his shoulder, and pointed it across the distance.

The flinch of Tucker's horse and the man's stumble had given Luke time to leap down from his saddle with his rifle and he was now kneeling. He brought the sights of the rifle into alignment and upon Tucker. He fired.

A fierce wind seemed to strike Tucker's shirt as the rifle bullet slammed into him. The lead projectile rammed him backward two steps. His bones seemed to melt and he collapsed upon the dirt of El Camino Real.

Luke leapt upon his horse and ran it toward Tucker. He had questions for the man, should he still be alive.

Tucker lay motionless upon the ground. After a moment, he stirred weakly and struggled to a sitting position. He looked down at the rifle lying close by on the road. He reached out for the weapon; his arm trembled with his great effort to reach it. He ceased the attempt. He coughed bright red blood upon the road.

Luke reined his mount to a fast stop, jumped down and knelt beside Tucker. He caught the man by the shoulder. "Tucker, you're dying. So tell me why you'd kill me for a horse?"

"Horse hell." Tucker laughed with a wet sound and blood gushed from his mouth. "Goddamn you," he said in a frail whisper. His body became slack, and his open eyes stared up unseeing at the sapphire blue sky and the vultures circling high above.

Luke was surprised by the man's words, "Horse hell." Those words, the way they had been spoken, made it seem that he had another reason to kill Luke. What other reason could he have had?

He went through Tucker's pockets. Papers in the man's wallet told that his name really was Tucker. It also contained nearly a hundred dollars in paper money. The leather pouch contained three hundred dollars in gold coins.

Luke would give Tucker's last words some thought. For now he would ride on to the hacienda of Armendaris and report the killing. Pedro Armendaris would know what action to take.

Luke pocketed the wallet and gold. He returned Tucker's rifle to its scabbard on the horse, his gun belt with the pistol was hung over the pommel of the saddle. He dragged Tucker's corpse to the side of the road. For the last act, Luke unbuckled the straps holding the spurs, with their silver rowels, from Tucker's boots and put them in one of the dead man's saddlebags.

He mounted, and leading three horses, rode at a brisk pace toward the Armendaris hacienda an hour of travel ahead.

***

Luke came into sight of the Armendaris' hacienda that sat on a broad, flat shelf of land that was an ancient terrace of the Rio Grande. The river itself was some eighth of a mile to the east. Immediately north of the house was a large round stone corral. The hacienda was a sprawling, single-story structure rectangular in shape and surrounded by a protective stone wall five feet high enclosing two or so acres. The hacienda was made of brown adobe, like the earth it rested upon. From the center of the hacienda, a round stone tower eight feet in diameter and thirty feet tall reared above everything. Luke knew, but could not see from his distance, that gun ports were located in the walls of the tower. From the most elevated position in the tower, a man with a rifle could kill any enemy that tried to use the wall as a shield while assaulting the hacienda. The hacienda was built around a spring that came out of the ground in the main patio, and flowed out under the wall in a channel too small for a man to enter. Beyond the wall, the water irrigated a large garden in the summer season.

Luke passed through the main gate in the unguarded wall and halted in the foreyard. On his left, two Americans squatted on their heels and leaned against the wall. By their clothing, Luke judged them to be Texan. Closer to him was a long hitching rail with three horses tied to it. On his left, a very old Mexican man was tending a bed of bright red roses.

Luke spoke to the gardener. "Hello, Gutierrez. "

"And hello to you, Senor Coldiron."

"I wish to see Senor Armendaris. Is he home?"

"He is in the main sala," Gutierrez replied. "With a Tejano, the boss of those two," he added in a sour tone and chucked a thumb at the two men squatting against the wall.

"Texans are a nuisance," Coldiron said, the killing of Tucker still heavy on his mind.

"Especially this one," Gutierrez said.

"What's his name?"

"Max Cleland."

Luke was surprised to hear that Cleland was with Armendaris. Perhaps Luke could now find out the answer to Colonel Munroe's question about Cleland's purchase of Mexican land.

"Maybe I can save Senor Armendaris from the Texan."

"The patron does not need anybody to save him," Gutierrez said with a half-smile and understanding Luke's joke. "But he will be glad to see you."

Luke, with Gutierrez's assistance, tied his four horses to the hitching rail along with the other horses fastened there. He crossed the compound, a patio and onward to the sala, the big central room of the hacienda.

Armendaris, a tall, erect man of sixty, was standing in the center of the sala with an even taller American, a heavy muscled man more than a decade younger. Armendaris was reading from a piece of paper, and to Luke, he appeared angry. Cleland appeared the opposite, relaxed, almost smiling as if everything was going his way.

The two men heard Luke's boots on the stone surface of the patio and turned to look at him. Armendaris raised his arm and motioned Luke to approach.

Luke continued on to halt a few steps from the two. "Good, day, Senor Armendaris," Luke said.

"Luke Coldiron, it is very good to see you," Armendaris said in a pleased tone.

"And you too, Senor Armendaris," Luke replied.

Luke sensed Cleland had stiffened at the mention of his name. He looked into the man's eyes and saw surprise in them. The Texan quickly caught himself and his expression became unreadable

"Senor Cleland, this is my good friend Luke Coldiron," Armendaris said in introduction.

Neither Cleland nor Luke made a motion to shake hands.

"I've brought your horses," Luke said.

"Excellent, Luke. I will look at them in a moment. First, I would like for you to read this letter that Mr. Cleland has shown me." Armendaris handed the paper he held to Luke.

Luke accepted the paper, and upon quickly reading it, saw that it was a personal letter from Sam Houston to Max Cleland and dated a month in the past in Houston Texas. The letter stated that President Polk had decided not to honor the titles to land granted by the King of Spain, nor those granted in later years by the Mexican Government to people in the New Mexico Territory.

Luke now knew the answer to Colonel Munroe's question about Cleland's purchases of Mexican land at pennies on the peso. That answer was in the letter in his hands. It could easily scare a Mexican land owner into selling his land at a low price before it was taken from him without any payment at all. He looked up from the letter and into Cleland's face. The man wore a smug expression.

Luke turned to Pedro and handed him the letter. "What is written here is a lie. Don't believe one word of it."

"What's that you say?" Cleland's tone was harsh.

"I said the letter is a lie," Luke said sharply, a hot anger rising at the man's tone.

"What makes you so damn sure it's a lie?" Cleland's face was rigid with anger.

"Yes, Luke, how do you know that?" Pedro asked.

"Because it's dated more than a month ago. And Colonel Munroe in Santa Fe received orders just three days ago that he was to strictly enforce the terms of the treaty with Mexico. It specifically mentioned the section of the treaty that states the American Government will honor all Mexican titles to land ownership. So that there wouldn't be any trouble with the Mexicans."

"You're calling Sam Houston a liar," Cleland asked belligerently.

"Certainly not, Cleland," Luke said in an equally hard tone. He focused all his senses on Cleland, waiting for his reaction to what was coming next. "From what I've heard, Sam Houston is an honest man. So that means some crooked sonofabitch wrote the letter and signed Houston's name to it. Now I wonder why a man would do that."

Cleland's face flushed with anger and his big hands closed into fists. "Why, damn you!" he snarled. He made a step toward Luke.

Luke braced himself for the attack. The man was big and strong and the fight would be a tough one. Still Luke wanted a chance to smash his lying mouth.

"SENORES! There will be no fighting in my casa," Pedro commanded.

Both men froze at the stern command. The seconds passed. Then Cleland abruptly turned from Luke and stepped to Armendaris and jerked the paper from his hand. He turned and stormed from the patio. A moment later, Luke and Pedro heard the rapid beat of the hooves of horses as Cleland and his men ran their mounts from the compound.

"Thanks, Luke. What you said is exactly what I needed to know. I will tell my people not to believe Cleland's words. But now you have made an enemy. A very dangerous enemy."

"I'd say Cleland has made one too," Luke replied.

"Yes. He is now my enemy. But there is a difference. I have my vaqueros. You are but one man while he has many men to take his orders."

"How could he have known that I was coming here?"

Pedro thought a moment. "Two days ago, when I first met Cleland and he asked to come and see me about buying my land, he also asked if I knew you. I said that I did. He said that he would like to meet you."

"I told him that you were going to deliver some horses to me in a couple of days."

"So that's how it all came about."

"What?" Pedro said with a questioning expression.

"He had a man named Tucker waiting for me in Socorro. Tucker tried to kill me this morning. He failed. I have his horse and some of his personal things outside."

"Why would Cleland want to kill you?"

"Maybe he was afraid that I might say something that would stop his buying of land from your people. Or because I shot one of his men in Santa Fe. My best guess is for the first reason. I doubt he cares much if one of his men dies."

Pedro nodded. "Where is the man's body?"

"About two miles north on the road to Socorro."

"I'll take some men with a wagon and we will haul the man to the officials in Socorro and explain what happened. I'll suggest they give the body to Cleland. If he denies knowing the man, then they can bury him in the town cemetery, and keep his belongings to cover the costs. As for you killing the man, I'll tell them that you are a good friend of mine and that I stand with you in that you killed the man in self-defense. They will take my word for that."

"Good," Luke said. "Where does Cleland live?"

"He bought a large hacienda on the Rio Grande just south of Socorro." Pedro fell silent, studying Luke. "I know what you plan, and I agree it is always best to choose your own time to strike an enemy. Be warned that he has many men and always travels with at least two of them. I would take some of my vaqueros and help you, but I dare not for, as your president said, there must not be fighting between Americans and Mexicans."

"I understand," Luke said. The man was known as a great pistolero in his younger days. Luke believed that Pedro even today would be a fine fighter to have by his side in a fight. "Come and let me show you the horses that I have for you," Luke said.

The two men went into the courtyard where Pedro examined the two horses Luke had brought.

"They are fine animals, Luke," Pedro said. "I am well satisfied."

Luke gave Tucker's wallet to Pedro. He kept the gold coins. He would give them to Cleland, just before he shot him.

Chapter Twenty

Charlie came awake in the gray, early dawn with the sun still hidden behind the far eastern horizon. He pulled his blanket tightly about him for he was chilled by the mountain air. He hoped it would be warmer on the lower elevation of the Plains of San Augustin.

He lay quietly and waited as the sun made its silent climb. Though it was not yet visible, its light was reflecting down from a high layer of clouds and was taking the mountains from the darkness. In the growing light, and within his vision a short distance up the mountains side, a flock of nearly a dozen ravens clung to the barren limbs of a dead juniper tree. He thought it strange that the ravens would roost so close to a human camp

As Charlie watched the ravens, the yellow eye of the sun broke above the horizon and its light fell upon the Gallinas Mountains. At the first strike of the sun's rays upon the ravens, they flew up in a black explosion of flapping wings and raucous cawing. They climbed upward and away, their strong wings seeming to scrape the rocky flank of the mountain. In but seconds, they were only a black smear on the distant sky.

"Noisy rascals," Ernesto said from where he lay in his blanket.

"Sure are. How about getting an early start this morning?"

"I'm ready," Ernesto said.

They rose from their blankets. With the same unspoken thought, they turned and stared at Magdalena Mountain lying to the southeast.

"If your uncle's place is where he said it was at the base of the mountain, then it looks to be about half a day's ride from here," Charlie said. "Let's go and ask him to help us find a good land for our rancho?"

"I'm sure he'll help us."

They speedily broke camp, and towing their colts, rode down the mountain side.

***

The bodies of two men lay motionless in the yard of the large stone house. The booted feet of one of the men lay in the water of the little stream that flowed close by. The second body lay almost on the doorstep of the house.

Charlie and Ernesto had ridden down from the Gallinas Mountains, crossed over the northern tip of the Plains of San Augustin and climbed to the house, barn and corral built on the low flank of Magdalena Mountain.

They now sat their horses and scrutinized the death before them.

"Damnation!" exclamation Charlie.

"Neither man is Uncle Carlos," Ernesto said. "The bodies are too big and their clothes are not something he would wear."

"Let's sure hope you're right."

"Uncle Carlos!" Ernesto shouted out.

"Hello, Ernesto," a call came from the flat top of the house and Carlos rose to his feet with a rifle in his hands.

"Hello, uncle. Are you hurt?"

"No. I saw you coming but was not sure who you were. Now I see it is you with your big friend. I'll be down there in a moment."

Charlie and Ernesto dismounted. As they walked toward the house, Carlos came out through the open doorway, stepped around the dead man and came to meet them.

His face was tight with some strong emotion. He spoke in a strained voice. "I'm glad to see you two."

"What happened?" Ernesto said and gestured around at the dead men.

"Five bastard Tejanos came to scare me into selling my land by shooting into the walls of my house. One of the bullets went through the wall and killed my beautiful wife." His face tightened even more and his eyes glistened with unshed tears. He hastily looked away from Ernesto and Charlie.

After a moment, and with his emotions controlled, Carlos turned back to Ernesto and Charlie and spoke. "That is when I shot those two men. The other two rode away. They said that they would be back."

"Do you know who they were?"

"I know who their chief is. That one there," Carlos pointed at the man near the door, "told me before he died. He didn't want to tell me but I convinced him he should." Carlos pulled a knife from a sheath on his belt. He moved the knife with the sun light glinting off the honed steel of the blade. "I peeled his skin an inch at a time until he spoke his chief's name, a man named Max Cleland. Then I do not need this man so I kill him." Carlos stabbed the knife downward as if into a body.

"Do you know this Cleland?" Ernesto said.

"He is a Tejano that lives in Socorro and buys Mexican land. He came here once and told me that the American Army was going to take my land and that I should sell to him before they did that. I told him that nobody would take my land. Then he sent these men to scare me so that I would sell to him."

Carlos's eyes glittered with hatred and he spoke in a low deadly tone. "They kill my woman and now I will go to Socorro and kill this Max Cleland."

"He will have men with him so I will go and help you kill him," Ernesto said.

"I'll go too," Charlie said. He did not want to go, but with Ernesto going, then he must.

"It will be very dangerous."

"Charlie and I have been in dangerous places before," Ernesto said.

Carlos studied the two young men for several seconds. "I accept your offers. Now tell me why you are here?"

"To start a horse ranch", Ernesto said. "We have eighteen filly colts and a yearling stud to breed them when they are old enough. Now we want you to show us the best land on the Plains of San Augustin for the rancho."

"Where did you get the colts?"

"We stole them." said Ernesto.

"Who from?"

"Luke Coldiron."

"I have seen this Coldiron in Santa Fe. He is known to be a tough man and will be hunting you."

"We know that and we hope he will not find us far out on the Plains," said Charlie.

"It is told that he has the very best horses." Carlos said.

"From what I have seen, I would say that was true," said Ernesto.

"I wish that I hadn't mentioned stealing to start a ranch." Carlos said with heavy self-condemnation in his tone. "Where are the colts?"

"Tied in the woods just down below."

"Bring them up here and put them in the corral until we return." He nodded at the nearby corral, made of stout juniper posts set firmly into the earth.

"All right," Ernesto said.

"When you have done that, hook horses to the buggy. They are in the barn."

"Yes, uncle."

"Now I will prepare my woman for the journey to Socorro. She must be buried in the blessed ground of the church cemetery. Once I have made those arrangements, we will go and kill this bastard Cleland."

Chapter Twenty-One

The sun had rolled down its high sky pathway and lay flaming on the far western horizon as Charlie, Ernesto and Carlos rode along the dirt road that skirted around Socorro. Carlos had warned the two young men that because of what they were about to do, they should not be seen with him in the town, and so he had led them on this roundabout route to reach Cleland's hacienda. Charlie was more than willing for Carlos to lead.

They drew near a tiny adobe house sitting close to the road. In a small garden beside the house, an old and stooped Mexican woman was digging potatoes from the earth with a spade. She heard the sound of the hooves of the men's horses on the ground and stopped her labors and straightened as best she could. She lifted a hand, so thin that the veins stood out in a crude pulsing network and shaded her faded eyes from the sun's rays that shone directly into her face. Carlos lifted his hat in salute to the woman and her age.

She stared at the three men on their horses silhouetted against the red evening sun. Her eyes flared wide with sudden fright and she cried out in a shrill voice. "I smell you, Death, I smell you. Don't stop here! Ride on!

Ride on!" Instantly she was moaning with fear and waving them on past her with swift frantic swings of her hand.

"We mean you no harm, grandmother," Carlos called in a gentle voice.

"Go! Go! Don't stop here." She clutched her breast, trembling.

The woman's great fear surprised the men and her words saddened them. They hastened on along the path. She had said that she smelled death on them.

Charlie considered the woman's words. Yes, they could have the smell of death for they intended to kill a man.

***

Charlie rotated the chambers of his revolver and checked to insure the firing caps were firmly seated on the nipples. There must not be any misfires when the battle begins.

He sat with Ernest and Carlos on the top of the bluff located some hundred yards distance from Cleland's hacienda. He thought it was a fine home, a sprawling, single level structure containing several rooms and built within a rock's throw of the water of the Rio Grande. A large interior courtyard paved with stone was visible.

The building appeared deserted, not even a servant moving about.

They had arrived but a few minutes before and tied their horses out of sight among a small grove of trees behind the hill. From their position, they could also watch the road leading from Socorro to the house. It lay empty.

Now they waited as the deepening dusk filled the valley of the Rio Grande with gray shadows. With the sinking of the sun, the day's heat was fading and the wind dying.

Charlie turned to watch nighthawks hunting in the darkening sky above the river. The nighthawks were nimble birds, gray in color, with streamlined bodies and narrow tapered wings spanning nearly a foot. At least half a hundred of them hunted within his view along the river. They darted and dove, turning on a wing tip to catch the night insects rising up from the lush vegetation growing along the river's edge. They called out with shrill shrieks as they chased their evening meal. They snagged the living morsels of meat from the aerial larder with quick mouths and swallowed them whole.

Several times in the past along the Rio Grande near Ernesto's home, he had seen the amazingly agile nighthawks feed with their wild acrobatics. He had sat on the ground as he did now and watched them dart and weave about through the evening skies and kill again and again in a frenzy of feeding.

As Charlie thought of the killing, the actions of the old woman and her crying out about death came to him and he did not like the feel. He shoved them away and concentrated on Cleland's house.

He came to quick attention. A man moved through the scattered bushes below him and a third of the distance closer to Cleland's hacienda.

"Look," Charlie called out in a low voice to Ernesto and Carlos. "There's a man down there."

The two hastily focused on the man.

"I see him," Carlos said.

The man continued a short distance onward and halted. He looked about himself and then crouched behind a bush and faced the house.

The figure seemed somehow familiar to Charlie. Then it came to him. "That looks like Luke Coldiron," he whispered.

"How can you tell," Ernesto said and staring down at the man.

"By the size of him, the way he moves."

"Why would he be here?" Ernesto asked in a worried voice.

"He wouldn't be hunting us here," Charlie said.

"He hides in the bushes and spies on Cleland same as we are doing," Carlos said.

"Maybe for the same reason we have," Charlie said.

"A man like Cleland who robs and kills will make many enemies," Carlos said. "If Coldiron is here to kill him, we must help him."

"I agree with you," Charlie felt the heavy debt he owed Coldiron for keeping him from being killed that day in La Fonda.

***

Luke waited and watched for Cleland to appear at his hacienda. With Luke having told Armendaris that the Sam Houston letter was a forgery, and in this way destroying Cleland's plan to buy Mexican land cheaply, the man would not allow him to live. Now, with a battle certain, Luke had chosen the place for the battle, the man's home where he would feel most secure.

The sun was hidden behind the far horizon and only a bit of its light still hung in the heavens. There was not one glimmer of light at the house, not a sound, no movement. He turned to watch the road leading to the house. He wanted Cleland to come so that the game of killing could end tonight.

As Luke watched the road, the figure of a rider and his mount, miniaturized by distance, took form moving through the grayness of the early night. The horseman fell into a depression in the road and vanished. After some seconds, he reappeared, larger, more distinct. The rider was still too far away to make out his details; still Luke saw that he was a big man. That would be Cleland, Luke judged from having seen the size of the man at the Armendaris' rancho. Where were the two men that Pedro had said usually rode with Cleland? Did the man still carry the forged letter of Sam Houston?

The rider halted at the front of the hacienda and tied his horse to a hitching post. He removed a saddlebag from his mount and entered the house. Shortly a light came alive in a window. The light vanished and reappeared in the courtyard. There it became stationary.

Luke rose to his feet and stole silently down from his hiding place and to the rear of the house. He moved along the wall to the back door, tested it and found it unlocked. That was not unusual and he felt no alarm. He pulled his pistol and entered silently. He immediately stepped from in front of the doorway and stood against the wall.

Luke cocked his ear and listened intently for any sound that would tell of the presence of men other than Cleland in the house. Silence lay complete. He crept along the hallway to the door that opened onto the courtyard and peered through.

Cleland sat at a small table made of wrought iron and holding a lamp that cast a pale yellow light over the courtyard. Saddlebags lay on the table along with a bottle of wine. Cleland, a glass of wine in his left hand, was facing in Luke's direction.

Luke, holding his pistol ready, stepped into the courtyard. The time for battle was now.

Cleland immediately saw him. He slowly placed the wine on the table and stood erect. A pistol was in his right hand.

Luke was surprised by the swiftness with which Cleland had seen him, and the pistol ready in his hand.

"Coldiron, I've been expecting you, and here you are Johnny on the spot." Cleland chuckled in a pleased voice.

A cold wind blew through Luke' mind. Cleland had anticipated his coming. What kind of a plan had he devised to kill him?

Cleland smiled broadly. "It's going to be good to see you dead."

"First, you've got to kill me."

"I plan to do that."

Cleland lifted a hand and a man emerged from a doorway on Cleland's right. At the same time, another man stepped into view on the left. Both men held pistols in their hands. Cleland had cleverly hidden men in the house and Luke now faced three enemies. Worse yet, they stood far apart. Never could he shoot Cleland and then swing his revolver fast enough to kill the remaining men. Cleland had devised a trap with no escape.

Luke heard the scuff of feet on the stones of the courtyard behind him and a chill ran through him. Another foe, no, the sound was too much for just one, at least two, maybe three were behind him. That meant he had absolutely no chance to survive. He dared not turn to look behind.

To Luke's surprise, a man came up on his left side and stopped beside him. He sensed other men lining up beside the first man. By the expression on Cleland's face these men were not part of his trap.

Luke cast a quick glance to the side. A middle-aged Mexican stood close beside Luke, and beyond him a young Mexican. To Luke's great surprise, Charlie Bell stood last in line. All three had their pistols drawn and were watching across the distance at Cleland and his men. Cleland had made a major error; he had used precious time to taunt Luke when he should have killed him. The odds of three to one against Luke had changed to four against Cleland and two.

The young Mexican said something to Charlie. Luke thought he heard the name Rosa, but that had no meaning to him.

"I have first claim to shoot Cleland," Carlos called savagely. "He killed my wife."

"Then shoot!" Luke ordered sharply.

Even as Luke spoke, Carlos fired. Equally quick, Cleland lifted his pistol and fired.

Cleland's bullet struck Carlos and sent him spinning and down onto the stones of the courtyard. Cleland staggered under the impact of Carlos's bullet.

Luke fired into the man on Cleland's right. Beside him, Charlie and the young Mexican were shooting at the man on Cleland's left.

The courtyard reverberated with the thunder of the pistol shots. The light in the lamp flickered and danced and almost died under the concussions of the exploding gunpowder in the confined space.

Luke swung his pistol to help Charlie and the young Mexican kill their man. His help was not needed for the man lay slack and lifeless on the stones of the courtyard.

Cleland was hard hit, holding his chest, and yet raising his gun to shoot again at Carlos. His movement slowed, stopped and he fell forward, his face crashing into the stones.

Silence lay upon the courtyard. Gunpowder smoke rose leisurely in the quiet air. Luke and Charlie and Ernesto stood unmoving, recovering from the shooting and killing.

Charlie turned quickly to Ernesto to see if he was wounded. Blood leaked from his left shoulder.

"How bad?" he asked.

"Hurts like hell," Ernesto said with a grimace.

Carlos's voice came questioning. "Did I kill him, Ernesto?"

Ernesto stepped past Charlie and dropped to his knees beside Carlos. "Yes, uncle, he's dead."

Carlos chuckled in a frail, but satisfied tone. "That is good."

"Lie still for you are bad hurt."

Carlos gathered his fleeing strength. "Coldiron, are you there?" he said in a frail whisper.

"Yes, I'm here." Luke knelt beside Carlos.

"Can you hear me plain?"

"Yes."

"Then hear this, I am Carlos Armentes, I am also known as Juan Alvarez. I give my rancho on Magdalena Mountain and everything else that I own to my nephew Ernesto Armentes and his friend Charlie Bell. They came with me and risk their lives to help me kill my enemy. Will you see that they get the land?"

F.M. Parker

"I will swear that's your dying wish."

"Then all is as it should be." Carlos drew a breath and exhaled it with a final whisper.

Ernesto cried silently. Charlie put a hand on his friend's shoulder and gripped it firmly. He said nothing, for what was there to say.

Luke checked Cleland's men. Both were dead. He moved to Cleland and searched through his pockets until he found the forged letter. Luke would give that to Colonel Munroe to justify the killing of Cleland and his men, and perhaps the letter could also be used to return the land Cleland had stolen from the Mexicans.

Luke turned to the saddlebags Cleland had carried into the house and lay on the table. He lifted them and found they were heavy. He undid the straps that held the bags shut and dumped the contents onto the table. Before him lay several thick packets of large domination American dollars and Mexican pesos, a pouch of heavy metal and a ledger. He up-ended the pouch and a cascade of gold coins spilled out onto the table.

"I'll be damned," he exclaimed. He had expected Cleland to have money with him, but never so much. The man must have many rich Texans backing his plan to buy Mexican land. They were going to be much disappointed with the loss of their money.

He picked up the ledger and looked inside. It contained a listing of ranchos and a dollar amount opposite. This would be the land Cleland had bought and the price paid. The prices were but a fraction of the land's true value.

"Who does that belong to now that Cleland is dead?" Charlie asked and nodded at the mound of paper money and gold.

"Damn good question," Luke replied.

"Maybe it's spoils of war," Charlie said. "Like down in Mexico where we kept everything after a battle."

Luke looked into the faces of the two young men. They and Carlos had saved his life. He owed them.

"Yes, it could be considered that since we did have a battle. Or it could be a reward for killing a thief who tricked Mexicans out of their land."

"We sure don't want to give it back to the Tejanos," Ernesto said angrily.

"We sure as hell won't do that," Luke said.

Luke laid the ledger on the table and began to divide the money into fourths, placing a bill on the ledger and then one in three individual piles. When he had finished with dividing the paper money, he divided the gold coins in the same manner.

Completing the division of the money, Luke looked at Charlie and Ernesto who had been silently watching him.

"We have earned a reward for killing Cleland and his men. This pile," he pointed at the one with the ledger, "is for Colonel Munroe and the army to use to help the Mexicans get their land back. These other three piles are for us. Do you agree?"

"I agree," Charlie said.

"It's a fortune," Ernesto said, nodding somberly.

Charlie began to take bills from his share and place them in front of Luke. As he worked he spoke to Ernesto, "Give Luke a thousand dollars."

Ernesto nodded and began to count out money and lay it beside that of Charlie's.

"What's this all about?" Luke asked.

"We want to buy some of your filly colts to stock our rancho," Charlie said.

"What!"

"Eighteen is the exact number that we need," Ernesto added.

"Well, I'll be damned," Luke exclaimed and understanding what was happening. "I should hang you for stealing them," he said gruffly. "But instead, I'll sell you eighteen colts and give you immediate possession."

Charlie and Ernesto nodded gravely.

Epilogue

President James Polk, using General Zachary Taylor and his army, contrived to start the Mexican – American War to obtain "Spoils of War."

General Taylor, after his victories at Palo Alto, Resaca de le Palma and Monterrey, was the most famous person in America. President Polk, knowing that the opposition to his political party was pressing Taylor to run for president in 1848, acted to lessen Taylor's growing popularity. He stripped away a third of Taylor's army and sent it to join General Winfield Scott in his invasion at Vera Cruz. In addition, Polk ordered Taylor to remain at Monterrey and not advance deeper into Mexico. Taylor released the men as ordered by the president. However, he ignored the order to remain at Monterrey and marched his now much smaller army south toward Saltillo. The famous Mexican General Santa Ana, upon learning of Taylor's move upon Saltillo, marched swiftly north with 25,000 men to meet him. Taylor arrived at Saltillo first. He quickly chose the site for the coming battle and positioned his cannon, cavalry and foot soldiers to meet the Mexican army that outnumbered him three to one. The battle lasted for two days.

Taylor's battle hardened little army defeated Santa Ana and he retreated south toward Mexico City.

Taylor defeated Polk for president in the 1848 election.

Polk died from cholera three months after leaving office.

Taylor died 19 months after taking office as president, possibly from arsenic poisoning.

For information on General Winfield Scott's invasion at Vera Cruz in southern Mexico and his march inland to conquer Mexico City, the national capitol of Mexico, see F. M. Parker's book, SOLDIERS OF CONQUEST, GRANT AND LEE, COMRADES IN ARMS IN THE MEXICAN – AMERICAN WAR, 1846-1848.

And interesting sidelight to the war—After the signing of the peace treaty in 1848, several prominent Mexicans, businessmen, government officials, and military officers came to General Scott and proposed that he resign from the American Army and issue a proclamation declaring himself dictator of Mexico for the next six years. A period of dictatorship would give Scott time to organize a government that would give the people what they rightfully deserved; a country where the law applied to all citizens equally, a true democracy, stop insurrection and the extortion and tyranny practiced by the military and the church. They also feared invasion from a foreign power due to their weak military and government in chaos once the Americans left. To seal the deal, five of the richest men in the capital guaranteed Scott $250,000 each for a total of $1,250,000 and the salary of the president for the six years. A huge fortune for that time.

Further bolstering the plan, about seventy percent of the American soldiers with enlistment ending would be discharged in Mexico. That would be some 10,000 soldiers. With a huge pay raise most of them would sign on with Scott. In addition, Scott could choose another 10,000 Mexican troops from their army. With that large of an army, Scott could defeat any nation that might try to invade Mexico.

After discussing the offer with some of his senior officers, Scott declined the offer, preferring to remain an American.

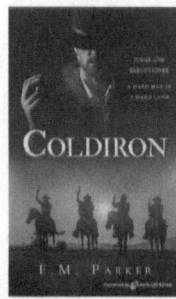 

Sign up for free and bargain books

Join the Speaking Volumes mailing list

Text
ILOVEBOOKS
to 22828 to get started.